"Yes?"

"I don't think you s

She sat still. This w is up. It wasn't even the first with those exact words. D me a routine part of each city. Not even each city—each ambush. Any time they coordinated anything with their Hawks, the revelry was always brought down by him.

"We've been over this," she said. She wasn't even annoyed to be having the conversation. It'd become so repetitive that she knew how to navigate it efficiently. "I'm not stopping. Someone has to do something, and I'm that someone. No one else is doing it."

"The Hawks are large enough now to do it themselves."

He stood tall, and at attention, his hands behind his back. It felt like a soldier relaying unwanted news to his superior. Which, truthfully, was exactly what he was doing.

"There's a lot of them, sure," she conceded. "But we both know none of them wield elements like us."

"I've been training them," he argued. "When you ... leave, each evening, I've been working with them. So has Teniv."

"And? A little bit of training isn't enough. Some of them have become proficient, but most of them will need years. Unlike the foot soldiers who got sent off to battle during the War of Fire, I intend for my soldiers to be prepared and to live. They aren't arrows to be used once."

"I never said they were. I'm merely saying that they don't need you anymore."

Rynara started. Luthier looked rigid, which was how he always looked, but there was an extra bit of tension in his stance that spoke to something else. Anger, maybe? She knew he didn't like her going off alone each night, but he'd never seemed that upset over it. He understood how strongly she desired some freedom after the way she'd been cooped up her whole life. Even if he didn't like her going out alone, he didn't reprimand her for it.

"Don't need me?" she repeated. "I'm not offended, I'm just confused. Do you not agree that you and I are by far and away stronger than the rest of them?"

"You and I, yes." He took a breath, then, with more emphasis, "You, and *I*."

Rynara stood, careful not to put too much weight on her ankle.

"Are you trying to say you think I should . . . what? Retire? And that you should take over?"

"Not retire. I'm merely asking you to consider entrusting us to fulfill this task and that you end your gallivanting."

"Gallivanting?"

He winced. "A poor choice of words." He cleared his throat, then brought his hands to his front. Not even up, or with his palms open. Standing like a regular person was apparently his way of showing apology.

"I can join the training," she said, still confused. "If you think that would help."

"That's not what I'm suggesting."

"Just say what you're thinking. I tire of the tiptoeing."

"I think you should abandon the idea of getting your throne back."

Rynara fought the fire building in her mind.

"Nobles never change," he continued. "They always accept bribes. They always want more land, or more power, or more money—"

"And you think that's what'll happen to me?"

"No." He shook his head. "No, I know that would never happen to you. But you've already suffered enough among them."

"I wasn't suffering." She scoffed. "I had hot meals every day and warm blankets and spacious rooms. I had the best tutors in everything. Anything I wanted to learn, I had it. I didn't have to save up to go to the academies or try and work while I learned a new craft. I had books and fine clothes and, and—and everything. *Everything.* And I thought myself in a gilded cage, simply because I couldn't do exactly what I wanted whenever I wanted. I was spoiled and selfish."

"And that's what you want to go back to?"

Rynara grabbed her head.

"No, I don't want to be that person again, but I want to right my wrongs. That's beside the point, though. You said I was suffering, and I was pointing out all the ways I wasn't. People kill—actually kill—to have what I had, and I knew that, but I still didn't really... I didn't really understand it."

"You didn't understand because you hadn't seen how other people lived." His voice was frustratingly calm. "Now you have. You've matured. That's good. You've helped a lot of people. That's good too. Now you can rest. Enjoy your youth. You always wanted to live your own life. You can do that now."

"If I do that," she countered, "then I'm just as selfish as I was before. I have to keep going. I have all the training my life of luxury gave me before, and if I do nothing with that, then what was the point? If people with a lot don't do anything with it, then the rest of the world keeps standing still. I can help. I can try to help, at least. Maybe I won't actually make a difference, but I can try."

"You've already done enough. Please, Gwen. You don't know what it was like."

She huffed out an angry breath. Schooling her features, she forced her shoulders to ease and pinched her nose.

Being hotheaded was part of what she'd hated about

herself before. She needed to at least try to hear what Luthier was saying before combatting his request.

"What do you mean?"

"I was supposed to protect you."

At that, he actually sounded emotional. Rynara felt her heart constrict. She'd never heard his tone shift to that timbre before.

"You did protect me. My whole life you've protected me."

"No. I didn't."

The look he gave her was one of reckoning.

She knew that look. He'd given it to her many times.

Where did you get this bruise? What happened to your wrist? Why are your shelves broken?

"Yes, you did," she said. When he opened his mouth to answer, she held up her hand, silencing him.

"You served my father loyally. You protected me. You did both those things."

"I did one of those things," he whispered. "I couldn't always do both."

"Get out."

He put his hands behind his back. "No."

"Get out."

"Gwenivere—"

"I said *get out!*"

He stood still. His chest lifted, and his jaw locked.

His feet remained in place.

Rynara shoved past him and opened the door. She stood behind it, motioning him to leave.

His eyes bore into her. She refused to meet them.

"I will ask Teniv to return," he said.

"Yes, see that you do."

"I . . . I bid you a good night."

He didn't say anything else. When he'd walked over the

threshold, and stepped from her view, she nudged the door shut.

    She wasn't angry enough to slam it. She just didn't like confronting that some of the things in her dreams were things that'd actually happened—and that he'd seen them too.

CHAPTER FORTY-SEVEN
RYNARA

It'd been three days since Rynara had ambushed the execution.

The city treated the event like a celebration.

Each night, people were drinking, dancing, and making music until the early hours of the morning.

Before the Redeemers had held it in a choke hold, Sarabai had essentially done that and more. When the Redeemers had started kidnapping people, however, or murdering or drugging them, jubilant spirits had been squashed.

With the Redeemers having taken such an enormous hit, the citizens of the city had chosen to be joyful. Not because the threat had vanished. They understood well that the Redeemers still had many of the city's enforcers under their thumb.

No, they celebrated in defiance. It was a dare to them. A challenge.

Try to take us. See what happens if you do.

Rynara felt mixed about it. On one hand, she respected and admired the fire of Sarabai's people. It was such a different city from Voradeen that she often forgot it was part of Xenith.

Knowing that two distinctly different places could belong to the same realm, let alone her realm, filled her with pride.

A person could be complex and multifaceted. Why couldn't a nation be?

She also found the wildness of the people irritating, as the Redeemers did accept the challenge.

Teniv and Luthier had ordered the Hawks to patrol as many of the celebrations as they could. They were running on little sleep, and those that'd been present during the execution were recovering from injuries, but from all the reports Rynara had received, they'd managed to fend off any additional kidnapping attempts. A few had even followed a group of Redeemers back to a storeroom. With Rynara's permission, they returned with more Hawks, snuck in, took the place, and gained a new stash of coins and cures.

Trying to work within the laws of the city, Rynara ordered all such findings be brought back to enforcers. They all knew many of them were corrupt, but some of the Hawks had infiltrated their ranks, and they informed her of who was pocketing the coins for themselves, who was bringing contraband back to Redeemers, and who was actually doing their jobs and handling the goods accordingly.

Rynara herself patrolled the streets too—once her ankle felt good enough to walk on. She'd fought off a group of Redeemers who'd followed some young people, but otherwise, she'd not faced much in the way of wrongdoing.

She'd hoped the tradesmen would be caught.

They hadn't.

Today, Rynara was finally meeting with some of the victims from the execution. They relayed to her everything they knew, some even going so far as to describe the faces of the people who'd kidnapped them.

"I've seen Navar," one said. "He looks like a kind man. Very sweet and small for a Prianthian. He's not the warrior you might expect."

Other than that, most had nothing useful to say. Rynara assured them that they *were* most helpful, and she told them how brave they were for being willing to speak to her after experiencing such horrors.

"You are the real hero," she told them. "If my family and my life were at risk, I don't know that I'd be as brave as you."

It had always been the right thing to say. Many of the people who'd come to her had arrived scared and timid. They'd left resolute.

They'd made a difference, even if the information they gave didn't get her any closer to Navar's main hideout. It was an act of bravery, and an act of defiance, to risk trusting her after everything they'd endured. It wasn't a lie—at least not entirely—for Rynara to say she didn't know if she'd do as they did. If someone threatened Aden's life, or Luthier's, and she couldn't guarantee their safety...

She honestly couldn't imagine being put in that position.

As for the people who wanted to join them, Rynara accepted all of them.

Not wholly. She told them they were accepted and gave them rallying words to lift their spirits and invigorate them, but it was understood by Teniv and Luthier and other trusted members of the Hawks that the new members were only to begin combat training, elements training, and weapons training. Other skills, like needlework, or metalwork, would be asked about and assessed, but the new members weren't to know of anything important.

Not yet at least. Hopefully in time, her circle of reliable members would expand.

Just as Rynara had placed some of her followers among the city's enforcers, the same could be done to her Hawks. It only took one Redeemer hiding in her midst to unravel all the work she'd been doing and all the plans she'd created.

"Is that the last of them?" Rynara asked, looking to Teniv. The two women were sitting in the back of the Moonlight Room, as they had a few nights before, though this time it was Rynara behind the desk and Teniv in the uncomfortable chair.

"No," the woman said, looking over her notes. "The other one is here."

Rynara glanced up at her. "The other one?"

"Yes. The dangerous looking one."

"Teniv, I have a question for you."

"Ask."

"Do I look dangerous?"

Teniv squinted, looking her up and down.

"You look small."

"That's not an answer."

"Sure it is."

"Are you saying small doesn't look dangerous?"

"No. I'm saying you look small. Small could mean dangerous because you have something to compensate for, or it could mean lacking in danger *because* you're small."

"Fine." Rynara rolled her eyes. "My point was simply that looks can be deceiving."

"I knew what point you were trying to make."

"Why wouldn't you give me a straight answer, then?"

"It seemed more entertaining not to."

Rynara fought the urge to thump her head on her desk. Between Luthier's overly formal nature, and Teniv's insistence on quietly annoying her every chance she could, Rynara felt like she was caught between two very large, very protective extremes.

"Just send him in."

Teniv smiled, uncrossed her burly arms, and left.

Rynara was sorting through her notes when the last man entered.

He was tall. Not so much that he needed to duck beneath the door's frame, but enough that his eyes took notice of its height, as though he were used to checking doorways before he walked through them.

His eyes themselves were all Rynara could see of his face, the rest of it covered by a wrap over his nose and mouth, and a hood over his hair. With the room's lamplight, she could make out green eyes and, despite how little of it was exposed, dark, warm skin.

She watched as he entered the room. His gait was smooth. Confidence poured off of him. Most who'd come to meet her approached with awe, reverence, or fear. Few approached her like it was *she* who'd requested a meeting with *them*.

She shared a look with Teniv. The large woman still stood at the door, waiting for Rynara's nod. All jest had vanished. Her broad shoulders were rigid, the veins in her neck and arms protruding. If she was hoping to hide her suspicion of the man, she was doing a poor job of it.

Rynara had been in Sarabai long enough to know it wasn't the man's Sadiyan blood that put Teniv on edge. People in the city coexisted peacefully, regardless of origin. Ryn wasn't so naive as to think the mind-set of Sarabai's citizens was homogenous, but if there were exceptions to the norm, they didn't exist within her second.

No, Rynara knew this man seemed dangerous to Teniv for other reasons. It was the way he'd shifted himself when he'd entered, so his back faced the room's corner, rather than its door. It was the sheer number of sheaths for *touched* blades he wore at his sides—sheaths that sat empty, thanks to Teniv—but that numbered well above twenty, by Ryn's estimation.

His clothes were dark and well fitted, snug enough to not

get caught or yanked on in a fight, but loose enough to not impede movement. They were adorned clothes, likely, and if they weren't, the vest he wore over his chest was.

Rynara was certain. It was almost exactly the same attire she wore.

"Thank you, Teniv," she said, leaning back in her seat. She fingered the *touched* blade at her side, both for her second's reassurance and as a warning to the man. Best he knew what she was capable of, if he felt like trying anything.

Teniv stepped forward, setting something on the desk, then returned to the door.

"Said if it made you feel safer, you could put these on him."

Rynara watched the woman leave before glancing at what she'd handed over.

Element shackles.

"Is there a reason," she started, eyeing the shackles, "other than your unsubtle appearance, that I should have reason to fear you?"

She thought she could see a smile behind the man's cover. As he pulled it down, and removed his hood, she saw that he was indeed smiling.

Then she realized she knew that smile.

She'd seen it when she'd tended his wounds after slaying the Behemoth. She'd seen it in the palace ballroom, when they'd shared a dance during the masquerade. She'd seen it when he'd come to her rooms, laying his soul bare, begging for her aid in retrieving the Dagger of Eve.

"I do have quite the reputation," Dietrich said. "Though I assure you, much of it is unearned."

CHAPTER FORTY-EIGHT
RYNARA

Rynara sat motionless.

She'd imagined this moment for months. Longed for it. Hungered for it. She'd felt his blood splatter her face as she slit his throat, tasted the salt of it as it dripped into her mouth. She'd seen his face every night before she slept. She felt his presence in every shadow that hung heavy.

Now that he was before her, she expected to rage. It was natural to let the fire in her veins pulse through her. She wanted to be set ablaze. She wanted to take the knife she fingered and release it, sink it into his neck, press it down deep into his flesh.

She took a breath. Steadied herself. Set free the anger. If ever she took her throne back, she would have to sit across from those who'd taken away her name, her knights, her father. She could not let anger control her, loath as she was to accept that.

"Dietrich Haroldson," she said simply. "Have you come to try and kill me as well?"

He gestured to the empty sheaths. "I'm ill-equipped to do so, if that was my plan. And trust me, Princess, if my intentions were to assassinate you, we wouldn't be having this conversation."

He said that with a smile too.

She wanted to burn it off.

"I'm not here to boast, though," he said, taking a step back. She could tell he meant for the gesture to be placating.

It wasn't.

"I speak truth when I say my reputation is only *somewhat* earned. I didn't kill the Laighless family."

"And the attempt on your brother?" she asked, tilting her head. "Was that an imposter too?"

He winced. "Well, no. That one was me. But the little eel was in on it, as was his friend Dorian, who is your friend too, from what I understand. Rare that, to be liked by so many. I'm always suspicious of people like that."

"You're rambling."

"I'm elaborating." He swallowed, a bit of nervousness showing, then leaned back into the room's corner with his arms folded across his chest, as if he could somehow erase any unease he felt.

She liked that he was nervous. She removed her hand from the knife and ran her fingers across the element shackles he'd brought.

"What proof do you have? Of any of your claims?"

"What proof do you have of yours?"

She stilled. "What?"

"Your father," he said, shrugging a shoulder. "I presume you didn't kill him."

She wanted to slam the desk, push it over, and watch everything atop it crash to the ground.

She settled for curling her toes in her shoes.

"No," she said through gritted teeth. "I didn't."

"And I didn't kill the Laighless family."

"That's it?"

She stood, still holding the shackles, and walked toward him.

"I've read every report," she said. "I've seen every story. You killed the al'Murtaghs, then the Laighlesses, then set Yvaine Barie free. She saw you, described you exactly, described your dragon. They found tracks in the field. Soles meant for sand, rather than snow. There were bloodstains in the house. The Laighlesses died just inside the door." She took another step toward him, shackles at the ready. "The killer didn't meet them on the field of battle. They didn't challenge them. They snuck up on them, from the shadows, and piled their bodies atop one another."

She sprang forward, ready to snap the chains closed against his wrists. Too fast, her body was spun around, the shackles on the floor, her back wedged into the room's corner.

Dietrich towered over her. His fingers wrapped tight around her wrists. There'd been a second of pain, when he'd bent her wrist and squeezed hard enough to make her drop the chains. Now his grip relaxed.

She could feel him about to release her, but she *called* fire anyway, a burst of flames igniting between them. He ducked out of the way. Some of the flames soaked into the vest he wore. The rest disappeared as she released them.

Heart racing, she grabbed again for the *touched* blade, this time pulling it from its sheath with a satisfying *shink*. Before she could throw it, Dietrich kicked the shackles up, caught them, then snapped them onto himself.

She froze. She still held the knife up, muscles twitching in anticipation. Dietrich held his own hands up, submissive.

Pleading.

"Instinct," he said, panting. "I'm sorry."

When she didn't lower her knife, he got down on one knee, then the other. He held his chin up, exposing his throat.

She rose up from the corner and slowly walked around him. She kept a healthy distance, recognizing his reach was much further than her own, then traded her knife for a *called* sword. She pressed it up to his neck, tilting his chin up higher.

"And if I tried to strike you down, would your *instincts* kick in again?"

He chuckled. "Possibly. I can make no promises on that front." He released a breath, shoulders falling. His mirth faded. "But I can assure you, Princess, I didn't kill the Mesidians."

"I asked for proof," she spat. "And you tried to plead your innocence by bringing up my father."

"Were we not both falsely accused? Not just with those deaths, but with the Attack of Fiends? Were there not rumors running unfounded as soon as the nobles righted themselves?"

She yanked her sword away. He released another breath.

"Is that it, then? Do you really have no other evidence to offer? I will not accept subservience as sincerity this time. If you offer me nothing more than empty platitudes, then I will have your head."

He didn't meet her eye, but he must have heard the conviction in her voice. He put his hands up again, nodding his understanding.

"You know I wanted the Dagger," he said. "Everything I told you was true. My mother was sick. Sadie was facing the threat of Redeemers. You see what they're capable of now. What they've done to the West. You're fighting them as I did."

She kept silent.

"We wanted to keep my mother alive. To keep my father sane. We never wanted to cause unrest. That was the whole reason we thought to come to you first. If I'd only wanted the Dagger, I would've stolen it from Roland. I'd never have tried to convince you of our plight."

That did, frustratingly, make sense. Not that she hadn't puzzled over that detail a thousand times already. She'd just been eager to ignore it. She wanted something to be simple. She wanted to believe that this one thing was clear. She wanted it so badly she was willing to accept blind hatred of something, or someone, if it meant she could have an unobstructed path between her pain and its cause.

"Do you remember healing me after the Attack of Fiends?" he asked.

She didn't answer.

"I know I have a great deal of scars, but I have others now —ones I got while I was at the Dividing Wall. The same time someone else was killing the Laighlesses in Mesidia."

He looked to her, hands lifting up to his shirt. She squinted, unsure what he might do.

Did he have more weapons beneath his vest? It could be a mistake—it was likely a mistake—to allow him to move further, but she nodded her permission. After how quickly he'd deflected her before, she knew he'd been right about her: she'd be dead if that's what he'd wanted.

Deliberately, as though trying not to spook a frightened animal, Dietrich began undoing his shirt and vest. Rynara backed up, one step, two steps, three, returning to her place in front of him, rather than at his side.

He'd been scarred before. She remembered that vividly, not just the fact of it, but the feeling she'd had, of something twisting around her heart. She'd been horrified at the sight of him, of a man so young, yet so torn apart. There'd been an elixir she'd used to heal what she could of his burns. She'd watched as the skin had mended itself, and he'd writhed in pain.

She remembered that, even after riding his dragon, even after entrusting it to help save her city, she'd been a little afraid of it as it'd watched over him in frightened anticipation.

What she didn't remember were the scars he showed her now. They looked too dark to be completely healed, too thick, as though holes still existed in his stomach, but nothing was coming out of them. They almost . . . pulsed too, not with motion, but color. They always stayed a dark red-black, yet somehow, when she blinked, the color looked more like a purple bruise, the blue of veins, or the green of something close to healing.

"My brother," Dietrich said. "When I gave him the Dagger, this is what he did to me."

Rynara's first instinct was to ask why. Or how. Her father had hurt her before—

She could imagine someone's relative hurting them. She knew it happened. A moment of anger. A moment of panic. A fear of what the world would do to someone if you didn't press obedience into them young. Those were things that, while irrational, still made a twisted kind of sense to Ryn. This, this obvious betrayal, this anomalous, dark, horrible act, was unfathomable.

She held her instincts at bay. For all she knew, it wasn't Dietrich's brother who'd done this but Pierre, Rosalie, or the al'Murtaghs when Dietrich had tried to kill them, and they had attempted to fight back.

Dietrich already had the Dagger by then, she reminded herself.

Roland had sent the letter confirming it. The only way it could've been them who'd done this is if they'd managed to reclaim the Dagger and used it against him, only for him to get it back.

It was possible, but improbable. She saw Dietrich during the Attack of Fiends. She'd seen him just now. She didn't think he was one to let a fight go awry.

"Directly after the Attack of Fiends, I didn't have any of the elixir left," he continued. "I'd used much of it to help the injured, and you used what I had to heal the burns." He absently touched another part of his stomach, a part that the elixir hadn't reached, where the skin was still marred.

"I came back to Sadie, and Seera, my dragon . . . someone had hunted down and killed her family. The Dividing Wall had been taken over by Redeemers, and Seera was too weak to make the flight from there to Sovereignty.

"I wrote to my brother, for him to find me—to bring an army if he had to—anything to reach me and get the Dagger back to our mother. I didn't know she'd already died. I'd been too late."

Rynara noted a shift in his voice. It was that same shift she'd been convinced by all those moons ago, when he'd met her after the masquerade and had told her his story.

She'd been so compelled to help him then. She'd wanted to do anything she could to help this man who'd saved her, her city, her family. Not solely to repay him or to fulfill some unnegotiated bargain. There'd been pain in his voice. Desperation. She'd have had it too, if she'd been in his place.

It struck something in her now.

She wanted to harden herself to it. She made an *effort* to harden herself to it, tired as she was for always being too trusting, too foolish, too inexperienced for the schemes and machinations of the world.

Yet the child in her, the one she couldn't kill off just yet, the one who believed good could triumph, wanted to trust that the person before her now was reaching across the void, baring himself, not because he wished to deceive, but because he hoped she might reach back in kind.

"While I waited for him to come, I hunted down the people who'd killed Seera's family," Dietrich said. "One of them, a woman named Brelain, was the person who'd given me the elixirs. After I tried to kill her, I wanted to take it back. I wanted to heal her.

"I tried, but she'd lost too much blood. All I did was . . . prolong it."

He cleared his throat, but Rynara hadn't missed it. That unnamed sign, whatever it was, that made it evident a person was speaking of something that haunted them. She'd need to understand who this woman was to him, what the rest of this part of his story was, if she was ever to really trust him, but for now, she didn't press.

"I stopped, eventually. I took what was left. I hadn't known she'd been with the Redeemers before, but after she died, I knew that I had to try and get the elixir to my brother. She'd said it didn't work on illnesses, but I thought maybe if Abaddon enhanced it or changed its makeup we could use that on our mother instead of the Dagger. I thought we could sell it too. Abaddon wouldn't hoard it; he'd use it to heal. It could do a lot of good in the world.

"I retreated into the mountains until he came. I couldn't hunt anymore, not after Brelain. When Abaddon finally arrived, he told me it'd been too late for our mother. When I asked of our father, he said our father wanted to take his own life. In Sadie, many believe that to do such a thing spells unrest in the afterlife, or a ceasing to exist. Abaddon took our father's life instead, to spare him that fate."

Dietrich's lip curled. He looked like a caged animal now, rather than submissive. Rynara checked the hold on her *called* blade, even knowing Dietrich's anger wasn't directed at her.

"I wasn't going to hurt Abaddon, but when he told me... I don't know. I've replayed the moment so many times in my head, but he did this to me." He gestured to his scars. "He thought I was going to kill him, so he tried to kill me first. He would have too, if not for the elixirs. I never had the chance to give them to him. I didn't even want to use them on myself, but after Abaddon left, Seera came to me and made me.

"He used the Dagger of Eve to do this, mind you. I don't remember if I mentioned that. I'd been quick in trying to be rid of that damned thing. It ruined my life. It led me on a wild chase for months—months I could've had with my family before they died. It ruins my life still, with everyone thinking I killed the Laighlesses."

He held out his hands, opened his mouth, closed it, then shook his head.

"This is it. This is all the proof I have. While the Laighless family died in a Mesidian shack, I was bleeding out in the mountains."

Rynara stared, running through his story. He met her scrutiny wordlessly, gaze expectant, questioning, but when she offered him nothing but silence, he looked away.

She watched as he brought his hands back up to his shirt. Mindful of her nearby sword, he cautiously began fastening his clothes back into place.

"The attempt on his life," she started. "Not the perceived one, in the mountains, but the recent one. You said that was you."

He looked back up at her, hope in his eyes. "That was me."

"And you said he was in on it."

"Yes."

She furrowed her brow. "Why?"

"To end the trade ban." He shrugged. He finished buttoning his vest, then made to stand, looked at her for permission, then followed through. She lifted her sword up, following his movements. With him crouched for so long, she'd almost forgotten how tall he was—how much he towered over her when he stood at his full height.

"The trade ban started because the West was treating what happened to the Laighlesses as an act of war. I was a prince of Sadie, and I—according to their accounts—ended the lives of Mesidia's nobles. If I could prove that I wasn't acting in accordance with my home, that Abaddon had nothing to do with my supposed accusations, then the West would see me as a"—he gestured to the air, searching—"rogue aggressor, you could say. Or one of the Redeemers."

"The trade ban is still in place."

"How astute of you to notice."

She almost smiled at that.

Almost.

"Things move slowly," was all she offered, but he was right. The ban should've ended by now.

"Things moved quickly when it came to enforcing punishment," he retorted. "People are quick to punish those who look different than them, who have a different culture, a different home, a different way of life. When it comes to forgiveness, people suddenly need time to deliberate."

He sniffed and rolled his shoulder, the chains around his wrists clinking together softly.

"Are you speaking about the trade ban, or are you speaking of us?"

The agitation seeped out of him. He gave her a grin.

"I was speaking of the trade ban."

She sucked in a breath, then *vanished* her sword.

"It could be both."

"Does this mean you believe me?"

"Not necessarily. But I believe Yvaine Barie even less. And she's currently in my palace, ruling my country alongside her daughter in my brother's stead. You're a *rogue aggressor* trying to do something from outside the throne. I'd say I have a little more in common with you than her right now."

His grin widened. "I didn't approach you simply to trade commonalities, fun as this has been. I came to offer my allegiance to you, same as many of the others. If you'll have it, Lady Gwenivere, it's yours. I can even kneel again, if that's what you fancy. Or I can cut myself in that blood ceremony of yours, if that's what you require."

"It's not *my* ceremony," she countered. She shook her head and waved her hand, a part of her wishing she could brush away the irrelevant defense. "No, I don't need you to partake in a Baptism. Based on what you said of your father's beliefs of the afterlife, and what your brother did in response, I don't imagine you're one for religion and tradition."

"What we know to be real is what should motivate us. Not stories of the unknown."

"Yes, well, I'm not here to debate or philosophize with you. I care naught what you believe, so long as you keep your word and do what you're told. If you're to serve me, that is what I'll require of you."

"Milady."

She wasn't sure if that was acquiescence or mockery.

"It starts with that," she said irritably. "You walked around as someone else for most of your life. You know full well you can't have people calling you *Prince* everywhere you go."

"Should I call you *the Phoenix*, then? I must say, I'm a bit jealous. All my years serving Sadie, and I had such uninspired names. The Shadow, the Assassin. By such logic in naming conventions, you should be *the Sky*, or *the Girl Who Jumps Off Things*."

"*The Jumper*," she countered, returning to her desk.

"What?"

"*The Jumper*. It's a better counterpart to *the Assassin*."

"It's all shit."

She laughed, surprising herself, then cleared her throat. "That's true."

"And if I'm not to call you *Gwenivere*, or *Lady Gwenivere*, or *Princess*, what should I be calling you?"

"Rynara Stone. Or Ryn. But I don't recall accepting your offer of help. What to call me might not even be a necessary point of interest. I still need to know if I can rely on you."

"Serpent and stone," he said, gesturing between them. "Well, Lady Rynara, what do you require of me? Perhaps a gift would assuage your worries? I happen to have the three runaway tradesmen you failed to capture during the execution. I managed to find out from them where the hideout is they've been operating out of." He examined one of his fingernails, tapped at it, then lowered his hands again. "Would you like me to lead you to them?"

Rynara fought the urge to grant any weight to his current smugness, but it took a great deal of restraint not to leap from her desk. Calmly, or with as much calm as she could muster, she took a parchment out, an ink and quill, and answered, "I'd prefer to leave you here, guarded. You can tell me the address, or draw a map, if you'd like, and I can confirm your word is true. Alone."

"Hmm." Dietrich squinted in feigned contemplation, then shook his head. "I'd prefer to take you myself."

In a swift motion, he yanked his arms wide, snapped the element shackles apart—or rather, the cheap material he'd passed off as element shackles—then smiled charmingly at her.

"You didn't really think a Sadiyan man would willingly put himself in chains, did you?" He slid off the cuffs and rubbed his wrists.

Rynara's grip on the quill tightened.

"Oh, and your guard is probably going to have a bit of a headache tonight." He walked over to the door, opened it, and stood aside.

Teniv was laying against the wall, still breathing, thank the Light, but incapacitated.

"You know all about that, though. Don't you, Ryn?" He crouched down and plucked out a needle from Teniv's neck. It was the same kind Rynara had found in her own neck when Dietrich had sent her back to her palace after the Attack of Fiends, when she'd insisted on going with him to face any additional threats.

She took a deep breath, held it, released it, then cursed.

He really could have killed her if he'd wanted. It should've made her fear him. Instead, very aware of her still beating heart, it made her trust him a little more.

It also made her feel a little sorry for Teniv. The woman would berate herself endlessly for this. There was no way Rynara could tell her what Dietrich had done, so she'd just have to wait until she woke up, lie, and say she'd fallen asleep on the job. Teniv would try to make it up to her, apologize profusely, or some combination of both, but Rynara would use this to make the woman rest. The Light knew she spent too much of her time guarding Rynara's back as it was.

"Was this really necessary?" she asked, walking over to Teniv and brushing aside the half of the woman's hair that wasn't shaved off.

"I couldn't very well risk her overhearing us, could I?"

Dietrich hurried over to the table in the antechamber to retrieve his *touched* blades. They made a satisfying sound each time he slid one back in its sheath.

There were even more than Rynara had thought.

"As soon as she comes to," he started, "and you've convinced her of whatever story you've chosen, you can meet me at the clock tower. You know the one, I presume?"

He gave her a wink, slid one last blade into place, and left.

CHAPTER FORTY-NINE
RYNARA

Rynara didn't necessarily consider herself a prideful person. She was perfectly willing to admit she had faults. If she was practicing the harp or honing her skills with a blade, she welcomed the critical eye of a mentor. Sure, it stung when she'd practiced a passage to the point of exhaustion, only to be told her rhythm was off. It was aggravating when she'd perfected the weight and footwork of a certain technique only to realize her grip on the sword was wrong. Yet how did one improve if they spent all their time arguing that their amateur self was not, indeed, an amateur?

Thus, if anything, Rynara considered herself an apt pupil. Humble even.

Dietrich Haroldson, however, had wounded her pride.

Walking through Sarabai's lamplit streets, jaw working, Ryn cursed herself. She wasn't sure why she was bothering to meet with him.

She told herself that if she didn't, *he'd* find a way to interact with *her*. Hadn't that been what he'd done the first time? All those moons ago, when she'd been walking through

Voradeen's streets? She'd thought she'd blended in so well. Who could possibly recognize her, what with how her father had kept her hidden most of her life, and with the simple garb she traipsed about in? So long as she'd hidden her hair, who could possibly know it was her? Why would anyone have reason to think the young woman admiring the jugglers and buying a mask was the heir to the throne?

Stupid. Stupid, stupid, stupid. She'd been stupid then, and she was stupid now. Stupid for letting her guard down, simply because her hair was dyed and the commonfolk viewed her as a hero. Why would she think that meant she could be at ease?

She ran through her interaction with Dietrich again and again. From the moment he'd walked into that room, she'd been a cornered mouse, thinking she was the cat. How had he done that? It wasn't as though he'd hidden his physical prowess and suspicious nature. She'd been distrustful of him immediately.

She was sure it had something to do with the shackles. Not the offer he'd made to put them on, which hadn't ended up meaning anything anyway. No, it was the way he'd reacted when she'd gone to put them on, like he really didn't want to submit. As though it pained him to do so.

Did you really think a Sadiyan man would willingly put himself in chains?

Was that it, then? She'd believed in that resistance, believed in that fear. But that had been an act too, then . . . hadn't it? It had been a gamble, resisting initially, only to give in after.

But it had worked. She'd known he was a threat, but she'd not been as on guard.

To sleep outdoors, she heard Luthier say. *You know full well a bug might be on your bedroll, but that does not keep you from laying your head down to sleep. Other nights, you will* see *a bug on your* bedroll. *If you're ever to sleep, you must find that state of mind from the former, and if you wish to kill all bugs who might sting or bite you, you must adopt the latter. It is up to you to decide: restful sleep, or peace of mind?*

She could live her entire life thinking everyone could kill her and would try to kill her. Or, she could accept that while she was always in danger, she could never move forward if she let that danger dictate her every move.

She was being logical, then. Yes, that's what it was. She was choosing to meet a man who had broken into her chambers twice when she was in the royal palace, who may or may not have been responsible for the deaths of her country's allies, who somehow seemed capable of talking to fiends and who'd found her yet again with no apparent difficulty on his end—and she was doing it all because of pragmatism.

You can just accept you're a dimwit, she thought. *That might be the most pragmatic thing of all.*

Dimwit or not, she wasn't going into this clock tower meeting unprepared. Which was to say she was about as prepared as she would be for any fight, with the added protection of a scarf around her neck, in case he thought to use any of his needles on her.

There was a little more armor on her person too, to give herself some credit. After coaxing Teniv to a nearby inn, and insisting she rest, Rynara had gone back to her own rooms, equipping additional protective items to her shoulders, thighs, and forearms. She still needed to be limber enough to climb, and a full suit of armor would've given her a conspicuous appearance, so she had to keep the gear somewhat minimal.

In many ways, she looked the mirror image of Dietrich.

A shrunken down version, but still.

She'd thought to bring Luthier along, then immediately decided against it. After what he'd said to her before, she hardly expected him to suddenly, willingly, and supportively accompany her to meet someone she knew she shouldn't. He already thought she should stop her gallivanting, as he'd so flatteringly put it.

She chewed her lip, still taken aback that he'd said that.

Was that all he thought this was? A young, foolish noble playing at heroism? Did he not see the help she'd provided to all these cities? Did he not see that, even without a title or a crown, she was doing good in her country? She was finally, *finally* doing something useful, and he wanted to shun her away again, just as her father had done.

Would he insist it was for her protection? When she resisted, would he yell? Would he hurt her, blame her, and tell her if she'd just obey, then maybe—

Rynara stopped. She reached a hand out to steady herself, the other clutching to her chest.

Luthier was not her father. And her father had done the best he could. He was plagued with memories from the War of Fire. When her mother died, he didn't know how to fight those memories alone. He feared Rynara would be taken, or broken, or used against him. He thought his enemies would go through her to get to him.

He loved me, she thought, pulling at the now-suffocating scarf. She took deep breaths, and when a few passersby asked if she was all right, likely thinking her a woman who'd had a bit too much to drink, she waved them along and insisted she was fine.

Righting herself, she checked that her Amulet was still safely tied to her arm, something she'd begun doing whenever she needed comfort, and slowly took in her surroundings. The alley she'd wound up in was narrow. The buildings on either side of her were a combination of stone and wood. The humid night made the material smell like she was somewhere else, the damp stones like those beside a river, and the wood like that of a tree with fresh morning dew. She found it grounded her, dead as the wood was.

As she approached the end of the alley and stepped back onto the street, she was met with people drinking and singing and laughing, some sitting on benches, whispering conspiratorially to one another, or flirting openly and confidently. Others clanked tankards together, spilling on either the ground or themselves, before hitting one another good naturedly and gulping down whatever they hadn't yet spilled.

No one paid her any mind. She sat on an empty bench, one of many that lined the road, and leaned back.

Listened.

Smiled.

I did this, she thought, knowing much of the merriment was the city's own personality come to life by its citizens, but also knowing this carefree celebration and joyful coexistence was the result of a people who felt less burdened.

How happy a person could be, simply by living without fear. She wished her father could've seen this.

She wished her father could have seen this, and known the part she'd played in it.

Would I have been so ready to spill over, so ready to leave, had he not hurt me when I was young?

Was she broken, deep down, from memories she'd buried? She'd thought she'd overcome the grief of her mother's passing. She thought she'd forgiven her father in those years after Rose had died, when all his pain—all his darkness and anger—had been directed, placed upon, or taken out on her. It would've passed. He would've stopped, eventually.

She'd known that. She'd prayed for that.

She'd convinced herself of that.

Luthier had seen it. Not the acts. Never the acts. Not before the last time, when her father struck her in front of him and Natalia. Before that, Gerard's anger had not come when others were present. Funny that, how anger could be managed when others were watching.

Rynara had wondered about that before. Then she'd quickly stopped wondering. If she wondered too long, it became obvious that it wasn't fair and it didn't make sense—that her father's love was conditional and dependent on his mood. His levels of stress. His state of mind.

Never her, she was starting to realize. She had never determined what he would do to her. It was never the fault of the prey when the predator wished to feed.

Was that the reason Luthier wanted her to join the people before her, become like them, share in their merriment? What toll had it taken on him, when she'd been younger, to know the bruises on her arms hadn't been from their last sparring session? To know the shelf of her bookcase hadn't been broken because she'd fallen?

How had it been for him, to know he could do nothing? How had he coped, knowing he'd been her protecter and had been unable to keep her safe?

What an irony, for her to be kept hidden from the world, when the danger was right there, locked away beside her.

At least Aden never knew Father like that, she thought, then surprised herself when her sight blurred.

She missed her father. She'd loved her father. She'd known he wasn't well, not only physically, but that something in his mind, in his emotions, wasn't right. How could she know that, feel that in her bones, know that in her core, yet be grateful, in some small way, that he was gone?

Why hadn't she confronted him, challenged him, for what he'd done to her?

He'd already harmed her: what more could he have done?

He could've become a poor king. His mind could've collapsed, and he could've tried to make everyone else broken, as he was, by way of his rule.

But now he was gone—and damn the rest of their world. She wanted to love him. She wanted him mended. Healed. She wanted him to love her.

She wanted the love from her father that she'd had from her mother. She wanted to go back to when she was young, when the world was too overwhelming for her to understand, when everything was both too large and too small, too vast and too narrow, yet her father's kiss atop her head filled her with warmth, her mother's hand running through her hair sent happy tingles down her spine, and the way they smiled at each other granted an unexplained security.

When was the last time she'd felt that way?

She supposed before her mother had died. Rynara's world had shattered then. *She'd* shattered.

Now she was merely picking up the pieces, unsure she'd ever find them all or put them back together the way they'd been.

Maybe that's all life was. Being broken down, torn apart. Reassembling. Picking which shards to leave behind. Leaving holes in their place.

Searching for things to fill the gaps.

A part of her didn't want to anymore. A part of her was done pretending she'd fashioned herself back into something that wasn't fragile, that wasn't about to break again. She wanted to endlessly mourn the past and the future that could've been.

Unbidden and obtrusive, a part of her wished she'd listened to that voice, that she'd jumped and hadn't *called* on anything when she'd landed.

Maybe that was the real reason she was meeting Dietrich tonight.

Maybe a part of her was hoping he'd put an end to whatever she'd become.

"Little lassie, would you like to dance?"

Rynara looked up, surprised to find an elderly woman smiling down at her. Her face was mostly wrinkles, a parchment that'd been hurriedly shoved into a drawer, pulled back out, then lazily smoothed over. Her skin was sun dark, and her hair a deep grey, but her smile was coquettish, belying her age. It seemed the kind of question and grin a young suitor would give.

"I'm afraid not tonight," Rynara answered. "But thank you."

"Here." The woman handed her a few coins, then gave her a nod and a wink. "It's too good a night to not enjoy it a little drunk."

Rynara returned the grin. "I thought it was bad nights that drinking was best for."

A shrug. "Bad nights, good nights. Maybe it's just all nights, eh?"

With that, the woman left. Rynara rubbed the coins together, the imprint of Xenith's rose without thorns tangible even through her gloves. Smiling, she decided she'd spent long enough feeling sorry for herself, stood from the bench, and headed to find Dietrich.

Sarabai was a wonder during the day, and a marvel at night. It was the brightness of the sun juxtaposed with the mystery of the moon. She'd been here for weeks now, and still, each time dawn arrived, excitement coursed through her, as though she were about to watch a flower bloom, or a baby bird take flight. It was odd, intoxicatingly so, to see a whole city lit up by small lights, little stars that twinkled from apartment balconies, round plazas, tavern patios. A massive collection of them were strung together around more notable places, including the clock tower, its face a rival to the brightness of the moon.

Ryn's cheeks reddened when she passed red lights, or deep purple lights, knowing those places were where more mature goings-on occurred. She'd been to a few of those, over the last season, finding them good places to get information. Still, she'd seen some things inside them she wouldn't be quick to forget. Perhaps they wouldn't have been so odd for her, had Luthier not being scowling from his place at her side. And, though she'd never really realized it before, she found she actually enjoyed how both the men *and* women in such places moved. When her whole life she'd been told her bloodline was central to her rule, she'd not really given much thought to what courtship would be like if she'd had the freedom to remove reproduction from the equation. She was relatively certain now that—if she adopted a phrase her mother had enjoyed using for art—aesthetic meant less than feeling. Sometimes what drew you to something couldn't be defined.

Sadly, though, she wouldn't be frequenting any of those establishments again for some time, and when she did, it wouldn't be for further . . . artistic research. Despite having saved some of Sarabai's people, there were still a great many risks that could befall them. The tradesmen who'd been pocketing coin for themselves and forcing others into servitude were profiting off someone else's web, and were sending some of the people of the city to places beneath it, within it, or outside of it.

Rynara was determined to find those people. Every city she'd been to before, every road she'd walked further from her throne—they had all led her here.

There were an almost endless number of routes between

the inn she'd left Teniv at and the clock tower. Assuming Dietrich had been watching her before, she chose to walk down a route she'd not previously taken since scoping out the city, one she knew was neither too open nor too closed off. She didn't wish to be recognized as *the Phoenix* right now, but she also didn't wish to attract attention from those looking for a quick pocket to pick.

Rynara noted that while Voradeen was still a larger city horizontally, as it granted its citizens large views that extended for what felt like eternity, Sarabai invited people to look up, to live in a different world depending on whether you walked the grounds, the upper pathways, or the rooftops. There were interconnecting paths in Voradeen too, ones that took advantage of its steady western incline, but it was more a charming view of something above, and thus, comparing it to Sarabai was like comparing a library that required a ladder to reach the top shelves to a library that filled multiple stories. In one, you could enjoy the comfort of familiarity. In the other, you could live a hundred lives, depending on which floor you found yourself on.

The city's design was a product, Rynara had discovered quickly, of Sadiyan influence. Sarabai had once been a relatively large city, though it wasn't internationally map worthy. It was integral to Xenith's trade with the East, but it never became much more than that, as trade with the East had often been a sporadic, inconsistent thing, and the eastern and southern points of the city led to the Forest of Fiends, which, to this day, people feared.

Once Sadie had been freed of enslavement and had allied itself to Xenith, many who'd wished to create new memories outside of the desert nation came to start fresh in a city that welcomed them, along with their knowledge of the best trade routes through both the Dividing Wall and the newly reoccupied Sovereignty.

While never having visited the Sadiyan capital, Ryana had seen and read about its architecture and the way buildings had been fit into the faces of cliffs or formed from the clay. They were built close to one another, with cloths draped from one rooftop to the next, to better provide shade for those walking in the streets below. Anything to keep people's skin safe from the sun or protect their eyes from the sandstorms that occasionally swept through.

That approach to a city, combined with the passion of Xen architects who often valued beauty over practicality and could not find many places to grant them both acceptable pay and adequate space for their work, resulted in a blending of styles, a fusion of old and new, of East and West, and opulence with sensibility.

It felt like a betrayal to Ryn, to admit she liked this place more, but perhaps it simply mirrored for her something she was experiencing in herself. Maybe someday, when she was old and her hair had turned white, she'd appreciate the peacefulness of Voradeen, but for now, her heart found itself wanting to discover more of this place, and more of herself in it. She wanted to see the way so many different peoples and ideas could innovate, argue, discover, and love.

Perhaps that was why Luthier had chosen now to beg her to stop. Maybe he saw the glint in her eye when she found a new part of the city to navigate. He recognized, no doubt, the longing in her when she watched people stopping their work for the day to eat food at a place they loved, drink imported wine in the balconies when the day's work had ended, and play music late into the night when the lights winked on. He saw the way she walked differently when she was not confined to her castle fortress or her palace walls. He saw that she could be happy here.

And happiness, she knew, was all he'd ever wanted for her.

I need to apologize to him, she thought. *I should tell him I'll consider it, even if he knows I won't. Maybe I should relieve him of his service. The Light knows he's sacrificed too much for me.*

As she approached the clock tower, she found her heart aching at the idea of Luthier no longer being by her side. He'd been her constant companion, the parent and the brother and the mentor. It was selfish, she knew, to keep him in service to her simply because she was scared to brave the world alone. He deserved to have a life separate of her own. She wanted him to be happy too.

Maybe that's what she'd tell him. Maybe he'd listen.

She knew he wouldn't.

The chiming of the clock reverberated through the plaza as it started its twenty-second bell for the day, marking the night's eleventh hour. Rynara was pleased at her timing, knowing that while the chimes sounded, none of her noise or movements would be noticed. She snuck around the base of the tower, first from the alleys surrounding it, then from up against it, searching for any sign of Dietrich.

She found none.

It would be much easier, she knew, to go up the flights of stairs inside the tower. Instead, she went to a building nearby, sprinting up the steps so she could reach the clock tower's tenth floor by way of the path connecting it to the building she was at.

If Dietrich had been following her recently, and if he knew which routes she frequented, he'd know from which locations she was likely to approach. And this—a dark building with red and purple lights—was not the way she usually came.

She wanted him to be the one who was snuck up on.

She counted the clock's chimes.

Three.

Eight more to cover the noise she was about to make.

Steadying her breathing, she crossed over from the building to the tower and hoisted herself up, grateful that this particular structure was undoubtedly built by a Xen. It meant there were plenty of things to grip, plenty of easily reachable handholds and convenient places to plant her feet. Xens did love their pointless embellishments.

By the sixth toll, Rynara had reached a small set of stairs, one with a ladder that extended down, in case the tower ever caught fire and the inner staircase couldn't be accessed. It was clear by the rust on the ladder that no one had ever come this way. Ryn felt a swelling of pride, knowing she'd likely found the least likely place Dietrich would expect her to come from.

Catching her breath, Ryn, as quietly as she could, climbed the ladder, and peeked over the tower's side.

She needn't have been concerned with where she came from. Dietrich leaned casually on the doorframe of the tower's main staircase, cloak billowing in the breeze. He held a rope that extended out and wrapped around the body of one of the tradesmen, who dangled from the tower's edge.

The other two, she noticed, were tied up in the corner. They both appeared asleep.

With only a couple of chimes left, Rynara hurried over to the men, found the needles in their necks, and reached to pluck them out.

She hesitated. What if they needed to come out only after a certain amount of time? What if she pulled them out the wrong way, and killed the men? They were awful people, and she wasn't sure she much cared if they lived or died, but she believed in justice, and she didn't think a cold killing on a tower rooftop, with them tied up and unconscious, was something she'd feel particularly proud about. Not to mention that these men had information on where the missing people of the city were, and she couldn't risk losing that opportunity.

One chime left. Cursing to herself and unsure what else she should do, she hurried to the tower's edge and grimaced at how the collected moisture seeped into her leggings. She repositioned herself to look relaxed, as though she'd been there a long time. She found the position she thought likely looked the best, propped her leg up, rested one arm on it, the other resting on the tower's edge, and waited.

The last bell chimed. The man Dietrich held over the edge continued to scream, the sound becoming much louder, or, more accurately, her ears registering just how loud it was, now that the clock had ceased its declaration. Dietrich stood from where he leaned and roped the man in, casually, like he was a fisherman pulling in a net.

"Still not enjoying the view?" Dietrich asked the man. "I'd have thought after doing this so many times, you'd have started to appreciate it. Have you ever seen the city from this high up? There's a majesty to it, don't you think?"

The man's reply was to cough, curse, and cough some more.

"Screaming is really not practical, friend," Dietrich continued. Now that he'd pulled the man back over, he prodded at the back of his knees, making him sit down. The ropes binding the man wrapped around his torso, making his arms completely useless and his balance shaky.

Despite the nature of how Rynara had found them, she was surprised to see Dietrich help right the man back into a sitting position when he'd fallen over.

"After everything you've done," he continued, "if anyone saw you up here, screaming in such a fashion, and realized who you were, I'm rather certain they'd encourage me to let go.

And unlike our Phoenix, I don't imagine you'd stick the landing."

He turned to her and waved.

Inwardly, she cursed. Outwardly, she lifted her chin, the most poised and dignified response she could think to give, and kept silent.

"My companion here," Dietrich said, pointing her out to the tradesman. "She's a bit less up for fun, as I'm sure you know. If you keep avoiding our questions, I don't think she's going to repay you with fresh air and a beautiful view. Are you, Ryn?"

She wasn't sure what to say to that, and she didn't believe much in her ability to act, so she settled for a simple, and hopefully intimidating, shake of her head.

The man, to her astonishment, started crying.

"I'll tell you whatever you want to know," he sobbed. "Please. Whatever you want to know!"

"Where are they?" she asked, hurrying over to him. "Where are the people you kidnapped?"

Dietrich offered her the rope, but she brushed past him. She had no interest in his tactics, not when the man was already willing to give her answers.

"I didn't do it!" he said, continuing to cry. Tears streaked down his face, and snot, both running into the thick black beard covering his jaw. His eyes were bloodshot and barely open through the crying, but she caught that they were green, a similar shade to Dietrich's own, though his skin was much lighter. Likely the son of a Xen and Sadiyan then. Not so rare in Sarabai.

"I don't care if you did it," she told him. "I care if you tell me who did it, and where they are. What do you say, hm? Are you going to tell me where they are?" She pulled out a small knife from her side, crouching down in front of him and holding it inches from his face. He tried to squirm away, but Dietrich pulled tight on the rope.

"Tell me, now, or you'll wish he'd dropped you over the edge."

Rynara had never intended to go through with her threat, but her voice and her reputation was enough to make the man tell them what she needed.

"Would you like me to scope it out?" Dietrich asked.

After interrogating the tradesman—whose name, she learned, was Eren—they placed him back in the corner with the two others. Rynara watched as Dietrich placed a needle in Eren's neck, then removed one from the second tradesman, placed him back under, then repeated the process with the third, each time confirming the information Eren had told them.

They all said the same things. The names of people. The deals they'd struck. The location of the people the Redeemers had taken and made into slaves.

All of it.

Rynara hadn't quite decided what do to with the information or with the men themselves. Dietrich had suggested they leave them there for the night, bar the door to the clock tower's staircase, then return, either together or apart, to deal with them in whatever way she saw fit.

She'd agreed. The men weren't evil, but they weren't good either. They'd secured their pockets and their safety by allying themselves with the Redeemers, but they'd done so, often times, because they had children who'd been sick and needed cures that, with the trade ban in place, only Redeemers could offer.

Eren himself had an elderly mother, one who had Widow's Wounds, an illness that only reared its head in women. It was manageable, but it cost a great deal of coin to treat, and that was only if you could even get the cures to treat it. The trade ban had kept even that from coming in, and while Xenith had some of it available within its own borders, the rarity brought the price up to a point Eren couldn't afford.

The other tradesmen had similar stories, just with different cures needed and different people in their lives who needed them.

It didn't excuse their actions, but neither did it make them deserving of torture. Which, loath as she was to admit it, Rynara knew torture was exactly what would happen to them if she handed them over to the people of Sarabai. The tradesmen had chosen their own families over those of their fellow man's. Ryn couldn't forgive that, but she could understand it.

She also understood that she'd set a certain precedent over the last few seasons of how one got to deal with those who'd wronged them. By going after those who were corrupt, and not always staying within Xenith's laws to do so, she'd granted legitimacy to chaos. While there were some criticisms of her acts in the various printings Teniv had collected for her, most had looked to her for inspiration or hope. She'd shown that while those in power did nothing, those without it had been transforming the country.

What she did now would determine more than she could likely fathom. She'd need to think through what to do with the tradesmen. She still wondered if she'd made the right decision before in handing the Redeemers from the execution over to the enforcers.

"Eren said the Sanctuary is miles outside the city," she said. "If you're to scope it out, I don't think going now would be wise. We'll go together later, after I've informed my people of this. I'd imagine with their tradesmen still missing, the Redeemers will be on high alert. If you go alone and get captured, I'd have no way of knowing."

Dietrich nodded and took a drink from his glass. She'd not wanted to stay at the clock tower and talk over everything with the men sitting there, even if they were unconscious, but neither was she ready to retire for the night, significant as the information was. If she went back to her rooms at The Tired Cat, she was certain she'd lie awake, thinking through all the new information, the implications of it, and what she might do with it, until the sun peeked back over the city.

There was also a part of her that wasn't ready to let Dietrich disappear again. She was finally able to speak with him at length, and she didn't want to throw the opportunity away. She needed to determine if she could truly trust him.

Hunting down the tradesmen had been a good start, but it wasn't enough. For all she knew, there was something or someone he wanted at the Sanctuary. Maybe he was only allying with her for as long as it served him.

With so much to consider, Rynara decided it best she and Dietrich discuss plans somewhere public enough that she didn't think he'd harm her in, but private enough that they could carry on a conversation without fear of being overheard. She'd picked somewhere that was much more alive in the late night and early hours of the morning than any other time of day, somewhere where the lights were a bit dimmer than in the rest of the city. The main area was filled with a mist, made from some kind of substance they put in the fireplace in the area's center. Most people, from what she could tell, came here to dance to the slightly out-of-tune music, get drunk, or do other things, things she wasn't sure were entirely legal. On the second floor, which looked down at the floor below, people sat in large, cushioned booths, where, upon ordering something to drink, you were generally left alone. It was a location of interest for Rynara that Luthier, when he'd first entered, had immediately, and without hesitation, declared, "I do not like this place," before insisting that they leave.

It had been one of the best meeting places leading up to the public hanging. It had also been very fruitful by way of information.

Dietrich, lounging back in the booth seat across from her, one he'd picked out in the very far corner of the upper floor, looked at home. She wondered if such a place was common in Sadie, but that question could wait. There were more important matters to discuss.

"Are you going to tell the enforcers?" Dietrich asked. His deep voice should've been hard to hear over the noise, but somehow it cut through, full, yet equally soft.

"I don't know," she answered. "Some of the enforcers have been replaced, but I imagine a fair amount still work with the Redeemers. If we tell them, they might do what they can to keep anything from actually happening."

She felt a hypocrite saying such things, given that she'd been trying to act at least somewhat within the law. The fact was, though, she didn't really know how to stick to said law, given those who were meant to honor it were the ones going against it the most.

"This isn't only a few criminals," Dietrich said. "You could find a way to alert those in the capital. Maybe get the information to those in printing. You don't have to do this yourself."

His expression was neither pitying nor expectant, but the words rang a bit too close to what Luthier had said.

"No," she answered, taking a bite of the bread Dietrich had ordered.

She wasn't in the mood for wine, like he drank, but after the day she'd had, food did much to calm her. The bread wasn't exactly bread; it wasn't flaky enough, and it was thin, yet dense, meant to be dipped in the yellow-orange substance the server had brought with it. Dietrich seemed familiar with the dish, so she assumed it was Sadiyan. She took a hesitant bite and found the creamy texture of the dip and the spiciness of it quite enjoyable.

"What is this again?" she asked.

"Meedla and sandmilk," he said, breaking off a piece for himself. "Not actually sand, obviously, but it's called that because of the color. Good, isn't it?"

"Quite."

"Better than that airy food you Westerners pass around at balls."

Rynara tilted her head, then smiled, remembering that Dietrich had been at the masquerade and had likely eaten the delicacies that'd been carried around on serving trays.

"That's not all our cuisine is made up of," she said with mock defensiveness.

"I'll believe it when I see it."

"Only when you see it? Chewing and tasting it won't be necessary?"

Dietrich finished his meedla piece and smiled.

"You're much better with words than you are at stealth. How're your leggings, by the way? Not still wet, I hope?"

"They're dry enough."

"Ah, dry enough. Just how most people like their clothes."

Rynara held back a snort. She was glad for the food she'd put into her mouth. She didn't want to give him the satisfaction of a laugh.

"I believe we have more pressing concerns than the wetness of my pants," she said. She grimaced as soon as she said it, but carried on, not giving him the chance to voice aloud whatever his currently raised brow was indicating. "The Sanctuary. I'm not great with dimensions. Do you know how big it is, based on what Eren said?"

"Bigger than this place and the surrounding places combined. Hence why I suggested notifying someone in the capital. Maybe some of your capital's soldiers could be sent to occupy it."

From the pockets of her vest, Rynara fished out the printings she'd gotten that morning. She flipped through them until she reached a portion on war updates.

"Xenith's army is spread thin as it is. Troops are at the western and northern borders. There was a collapse in the valley here that some are saying was a result of some kind of natural disaster, but most suspect it was some kind of attack. Natalia isn't going to bring troops in from there to come here.

"And here in Mesidia?" She indicated a place on the printing. "Xenith has deployed troops to help keep the Lost Elite from taking control of key areas, and given it's Natalia's home country, I don't suspect she's going to pull any soldiers from there, either."

Dietrich leaned forward, looking through the printing. His hand covered his mouth, the motion making him look decidedly less intimidating, especially when a small line appeared between his brows.

She scooted the papers around and over toward him, granting him a better view, then took a few more bites of the meedla and sandmilk.

He looked older than when she'd first met him. His eyes had a tiredness to them, as though he hadn't slept well in years. Stubble lined his jaw, except where a small scar on the side kept the hair from growing through. A similar one cut through his brow. His hair, which had been cut short before, now hung longer. Becca would've loved working with it. She always complimented Rynara for how thick her hair was. Ryn could only imagine the joy her chambermaid would feel running her hands through his.

"Perhaps your right," he said. "I thought there might be something here." He took his own turn poking the printing. "They've started this program to employ more knights, but it looks like the majority of those joining are children starting out as squires. I don't imagine siccing an army of adolescents on the Redeemers will do much good."

"What of your dragon?" she asked quietly. "Seera."

"She could help," he said, passing the printings back over. "But we'd also run the risk of archers or crossbowmen shooting her down from what is essentially a fortress. Until we take a look at it, I won't be able to assess how much help Seera will be or if I can risk her at all."

"Of course."

"If she even agrees to help, that is. She can be a bit strong-headed, that one."

"Mm."

"She liked you, though."

Rynara, despite not understanding how Dietrich could

communicate with a dragon, found herself sitting a little taller at the statement.

"Oh?"

"I did just say she's strongheaded. Shouldn't be a mystery why she'd find a kindred spirit in you."

"I'm not sure if that's meant as an insult, a compliment, or some form of both."

Dietrich grinned. "I suppose it depends on who you're asking."

"Well I'm asking no one, and it matters little." She motioned for the wine, finding the sandmilk sticking in her throat. Dietrich obliged, handing the glass over. He was clearly waiting for her to give it back when she finished, but she made a point of keeping it on her side of the table. She wasn't sure what point she was making. She just wanted some small victory.

At least his dragon liked her.

"I think we'll get nowhere," he continued, "so long as we don't know much about the Sanctuary. We can plan all night, but if the place is made of wood instead of stone, or if it's well guarded or relying on its hidden location, it'll effect whatever ideas we come up with."

"I... I agree."

"But we shan't be too discouraged. We gained valuable information tonight. I'm sure a night's rest and the ideas of your comrades will help us come up with an effective plan. I'll keep the tradesmen somewhere safe for the time being so if we need to speak with them again or confirm anything after we go to the Sanctuary, we can ask them."

"Thank you. That's—that's very helpful."

Dietrich paused, eyeing her. "Is there something else?"

"I want to go tomorrow," she said. "If I wait to tell everyone else, we'll just talk in circles, as you and I are doing now. At least if we go, we can relay more specific information back to them and then actually be able to make progress in the way of planning."

She thought, at first, that Dietrich didn't approve of the idea. She wasn't sure why; he'd been perfectly willing to find the place tonight, late as it was, before she'd objected to the idea. By the way he looked at her now, though, face seemingly devoid of thought, she wished she could pierce through his skull and puzzle out what his expression meant.

"We go tomorrow then," he said. He reached across the table and took his wine back, drinking what was left of it. When she gave him a quick glare, he said, "Wouldn't want a small person like yourself incapable of walking when we have such an important day tomorrow. Not to mention, this was mine."

"You're right," she said, scooting the food his way. "You can finish that too. I'll head back to where I'm staying, and you can meet me there, at ... how about the fourth chime?"

Dietrich nearly choked on his food. "Fourth?"

"Do you not do well on little sleep?"

"I do perfectly well on little sleep." He brushed his hands over the meedla basket. "It's the hour you've suggested. I don't believe in anything holy, but I'm rather certain even the Creator finds such hours evil."

Rynara stared. "Are you being difficult, or are you being serious?"

"Are you being serious?"

"Why would I jest about this?"

Dietrich held out his hands. "Because ... it's so early."

Rynara couldn't help herself. She laughed. "I've always risen early. Though I suppose, given your reputation, you were more a person of the night?"

"Well, yes, though I'd word it differently. The way you say it makes it sound as though I got paid to—"

"Yes, yes. I heard it. Point is, we evidently function best at different hours. You offered your allegiance to me, though, remember? And I say the fourth chime. I'll retract what I said of our meeting place, though. I'd rather meet you where you're staying. That way, the prissy noble that you are, you can get more sleep."

"I've slept on many a rooftop and in many a stable, I'll have you know."

"That's lovely. Where are you staying?"

At this, Dietrich had the decency to look sheepish.

"I'm staying where you're staying."

Rynara sighed. "Of course you are. And your room? Am I going to discover you've been staying in my closet or under my bed? Inside the chest at the foot of the bed, perhaps?"

"No," Dietrich said with feigned insult. "I'm in the room across from yours."

"Ah. Much better."

"If the options are in the same room as you or in my own room, I daresay it is, in fact, much better."

"It's not the best."

He pointed at her smugly. "I'm a very thorough man."

"You're a very thorough stalker."

"Fine, yes, I've not approached you with the most conventional of methods." He raised his hand in surrender. "But you have to admit, it'll be nice in the morning to not have to go anywhere to meet with me."

"That is not a very strong argument for stalking."

"I'd appreciate if you'd stop calling it that."

"I'd appreciate if you'd stop doing it."

He raised his hands higher. "I concede. Now, if you're finished with this food, I think it best we head back to the inn we both happen to, very conveniently, be staying at, and get some rest. This horrible woman I'm an associate of is making us wake up at the fourth toll. I know, I know, you're thinking, 'Ah, what a dreadful woman she must be to make you rise at such an awful hour,' but fear not, she is not altogether terrible—"

"Please," Rynara said, this time taking her turn to hold up surrendering hands. "Given the fatigue I'm feeling and the endless prattling you're apparently capable of, I think it's very clear that you have your energy now, and I have mine early. Can we please, without comment, get going?"

With a smile and one last bite of food, Dietrich wordlessly gestured, paid the server before leaving, and quietly followed her back to the inn.

CHAPTER FIFTY
DIETRICH

Dietrich was not woken by the fourth chime of the clock. He was woken by four knocks at his door.

He pulled his blanket over his head and cursed. He'd been grateful for a lot of things the last few days—finding Gwenivere, capturing the tradesmen, getting answers from them, having Gwenivere tentatively believe him—but right then, after so little sleep, and the sky still dark because of morning, *morning*, dammit, *not* night, he thought it might just be better to curl up and die.

"I know this is your room," Gwenivere said, her voice far too chipper. "You made the very grievous error of becoming lazy in your stalking and wanting a room right across from mine."

He clutched the blanket tighter. For a very brief, very fleeting second, he wondered if he could possibly just put a needle in her neck, drag her into his room, and go back to sleep.

"Fourth chime will happen any moment now," she continued. "Honestly, the ears start to tune it out, so I figured it would be most prudent for me to—"

Dietrich sprang from his bed, threw on his trousers, and opened the door.

"Come to your room and . . ."

Given their height difference, opening the door meant she was level with his chest. Her eyes immediately darted upward.

"Apologies," she said, clearing her throat. "I assumed you'd be dressed."

"Ryn, unless I have a spectacular bosom I wasn't aware of, I don't think it matters much if you see this."

Rynara shrugged. "Depends on who's looking."

"You just saw it yesterday. Remember? I showed you the scars."

"That was different."

"How?"

"You hadn't just woken up."

He leaned on the doorframe, crossing his arms.

"So all those snide remarks about me being overly talkative was hypocrisy, I gather? Because it seems you're rather capable of it yourself."

Her momentary embarrassment vanished.

"Sounds like you're up. I'll meet you outside."

Dietrich groaned, closed the door on her, and grabbed his shirt.

It was another twenty minutes before the chimes started.

As he descended the inn's steps, the woman at the front tilted her head, surprised as he muttered a low and disgruntled, "Morning."

"Ah, good morning to you as well, good gentleman!"

Dietrich furrowed his brow and shook his head.

There was something wrong with people who had such constitutions.

"You know," he said, walking up to Gwenivere. She was standing under a tree outside, the lights hanging from its branches still aglow. They shone a soft pink, and if he squinted, he swore he could see her short hair red again, rather than the color it currently was.

"I'm not really one to believe in deities," he continued. "Though I think I might now."

"Oh?" She handed him something. Food, he realized, by the smell and the warmth. He unfolded the wrapping and found himself nearly drooling.

He had no idea where she'd managed to get a cooked turkey leg so early, but his stomach was nearly empty, and the smell was divine.

"Yes," he said, taking a bite. "See, there are certain hours of the day that humans are meant to function. This hour is not one of them. The only explanation that makes sense to me is that there are, in fact, deities, and you worship an evil one. These are its hours."

She uncurled her own wrapping and started walking. He followed behind, savoring the food's taste.

"You caught me," she said. "I'm actually attempting to convert you."

"It's not working."

"Perhaps after you see the human sacrifice. That's what I've been doing with Redeemers I've captured, actually."

"That might entice me."

She chuckled, though her mouth was full, and she had to cover it to ensure no food came out.

Dietrich stared down at her, surprised. He'd not thought a pampered princess who'd been kept in her father's castle most of her youth would find grim jests amusing. In truth, he'd expected she'd blanch at the idea.

You saw how she fought against the Behemoth, he thought. *And you saw her bite a man's ear off at the execution.*

I don't think a very light dose of the macabre is going to send her running.

They walked in silence for a time, which was fine by him. His mind hadn't fully started functioning. The food was helping, though, as was the crisp chill of morning. Present company helped too. For how short she was, Gwenivere kept a brutal pace.

Sarabai was large, and by the time they'd finished their food and reached the outskirts, the sun had just started rising. Slowly the lights of the city began to dim, replaced by a single radiant glow of gold. Dietrich stopped for a moment, taking it in.

Gwenivere seemed to notice he was no longer at her side and halted.

"What is it?" she asked. Smiling, she tucked her hands into the pockets of her jacket. "Never seen the sun in the morning?"

He smiled back, but it fell quickly.

"Something like that."

She stepped closer. "Care to elaborate?"

He let out a slow breath, watching as it clouded in front of him. It reminded him of Seera after she breathed flames.

Is the cold bothering you, old girl? he asked, dropping his shields.

The dragon sent back an image of the mountain peaks she rested in a few hours outside the city and the fire she'd made for herself to keep warm.

Be glad I didn't let you wallow in sadness, and leave me be, she said. *Don't you have a princess to talk to now?*

Dietrich closed off the connection and turned to Gwenivere. Her teal eyes looked shockingly bright in the morning light.

His chest coiled up and tightened.

"The last time I saw my mother alive, it was sundown," he said. "And yes, though you were mocking me, I haven't really watched a sunrise since she and my father died. Only more sunsets."

"There's something different about dawn," she replied. He expected her to tease him more, but her voice had taken on a softer, almost reverent tone.

"Twilight is twilight," she continued. "It should all be the same. The colors are the same. The concept is the same. It's not, though. One marks the end of the day, and the other marks the beginning. Dawn is . . . different."

She pulled the scarf she wore from her neck and tucked it into her satchel.

"That's how I've always seen it anyway."

"I think you just described the literal difference between dusk and dawn."

She gave him a flat stare.

"Sorry. I'm not normally so insufferable."

The stare became flatter.

"All right, I am often insufferable. And you're correct; it does mark something different. I've been in a state of . . . I'm not sure. Denial? Misery? I've been in that state so long that I'd numbed myself to the idea of what came next. After what happened with my brother, I knew that was an end. I didn't expect to feel a beginning again."

He grimaced. Generally, he didn't embarrass easily, but the words had tumbled out of him, and from an unexpectedly wounded place.

He felt a fool. He wasn't sure he'd even made sense.

"I understand," Gwenivere said, stepping closer. "I think I'm currently in that state."

Dietrich stared at the sunrise, admiring the scattered rays

settling onto Sarabai's streets. When he tore his eyes away, he looked down, studying Gwenivere. He'd never known a person to shift between extremes so quickly. Hot, then cold. Annoyance, then compassion. Anger, then contemplation.

He wondered if she ever operated between those two extremes. He wondered if she even knew how.

"Have you found your new beginning yet?" he asked.

At her side, her gloved hands opened and closed. Likely to keep the morning from numbing them, though Dietrich suspected it was something more.

"I'm trying."

She met his eyes and smiled lightly.

"You've brought a new beginning to a lot of people," he said, gesturing to the city. "You're going to bring a lot more if we find the Sanctuary and liberate it."

She nodded. "I know."

"Maybe you'll find your new beginning along the way."

She smiled again, but it was more fleeting than the last.

"We should get going," she said. "Especially if we're going to make that human sacrifice." She punched his shoulder lightly. "Wait too long and the sacrifice will be to the wrong god."

"Ah, of course. Apologies, good servant of darkness. The light was trying to steal me away from your grim and gruesome path."

Her eyes crinkled. She picked up her brutal pace again—more brutal, actually, as it was faster than it'd been before—and though it was still far too early and too quiet for his liking, Dietrich found he didn't completely loathe everything about the morning.

THE TIRED CAT had already been rather close to the edges of Sarabai, but it'd been further east in the city when Dietrich and Gwenivere needed to go the opposite direction.

According to tradesmen's directions, the Sanctuary was within the West's side of the Dividing Wall. Unlike the caves in Sadie, which were twisting, narrow things, like the hollowed-out body of a serpent, the Xen side contained large chambers and fractures in the ceilings to let in light. Rather than elemental metal, the West's caves had mushrooms and plants, some big enough to dwarf even a small house, while others were the size of one's fingernails.

The different makeups of the plants made it too challenging to settle, as some were soft and of a good enough taste to eat while others released pollutants that could end someone's life.

Expeditions had taken place over the centuries, when people had discovered the treasure of wealth on the East's side and had hoped to find the same in the West. After a number of failed attempts, and a trail of dead bodies, the caves had been deemed uninhabitable, dangerous, and useless.

Rynara recalled finding something as a child that described them.

"The Cave of Death and Dreams," she said. "I'm rather certain that's what the book called it. It was so long ago that I think I'd categorized it as fiction. Hard to believe the place is actually real."

"I'd heard of it too," he said. "Though in Sadiyan stories, it was called the Serpent's Breath."

Gwenivere seemed on edge, so he added, "My brother and I would call it the Serpent's Farts."

She laughed, then rubbed her arms. The sun had fully risen hours ago, so the motion clearly wasn't from the cold. Besides, she had her scarf and the jacket she'd taken off and thrown into her pack. If her body did suddenly need warmth, she had full access to it.

"Rynara?"

"Hm?"

"Are you afraid of caves?"

"No."

"Are you afraid of the dark?"

"No."

"Are you afraid of poisonous plants?"

She swallowed.

"No."

"Ah, you are afraid of them."

"Well it's not natural. Plants shouldn't be emitting things that can kill people. What's the point? It's not like they can eat us."

"That's true. It would be much better if they could eat us."

She stopped, and he nearly bumped into her.

"They can't, can they?"

He shrugged.

"It would be more natural if they did, right?"

She grumbled and stormed off. Amused, he plucked a flower from the ground, and tucked it into his pocket.

The closer to the mountain base they got, the more the land around them shifted from open fields to tight, closed-in forests. The trees were not large, but they were packed close together, enough that their canopies blotted out the sun.

Cold met them as they crossed into the thicket. The morning dew that could be seen on blades of grass was suddenly puddled on the ground beneath them, turning the firm dirt into soft soil.

Small blooms littered the entire grove. Like the lamps of Sarabai, the blooms glowed, those among the treetops a green-teal, a lighter counterpart to the color of Gwenivere's eyes, while the floor was littered with tiny pink blossoms. The bulbs even hung like lanterns, their stems bent from the weight, and the petals opening toward the ground.

It was possibly the most beautiful place Dietrich had ever seen. And, given the ominous warnings of danger across the posts just before the area, it seemed relatively unmarked by human hands.

Curious what she thought, Dietrich looked to Gwenivere, worried she might still be afraid.

Her eyes had alighted. She slowly spun around, taking everything in, as though she were a child only just now seeing the sky.

"Breathtaking, isn't it?"

He nodded.

"Just the word I was thinking."

They were careful where they stepped after that. Neither wanted to be the one to squash the flowers' lights, though with how many there were, it was difficult not to. They winced each time the pink lights winked out, and though they lost a great deal of time with their newly mindful trek, Dietrich didn't care. The day was meant to be reconnaissance, after all. They were in no hurry.

Reaching a clearing, he and Gwenivere stopped, finding a patch of grass that didn't contain as many flower bulbs, and sat to rest. She pulled out some food and water from her satchel, and they ate quietly, both continuing to admire the forest around them. They were also both ravenous, despite the food she'd provided earlier. Five hours of straight walking and hiking did tend to have that effect.

"How many canteens of water are in that pack?" Dietrich asked, noting as she put her second of the day—now empty—back in, and pull out a third. She'd already given him two, which had to mean there'd been at least five full ones when they'd started.

"Ten," she answered. "Five for each of us."

He reached over and grabbed the pack, and though she protested a little, she gave up quickly.

"I'll carry this from here on out."

"Can I have my scarf for a bit? And my jacket?"

He pulled the clothes out and handed them over. She thanked him, then bundled them up and made a makeshift pillow.

"Did you sleep at all last night?" he asked, watching her rest her head and sigh contentedly.

"No," she answered, closing her eyes. "It made more sense to stay up."

From his own satchel, Dietrich pulled out a small flask.

"Here. This'll help."

She opened an eye, studying the canteen. As she took it, she propped herself on her elbow, unscrewed the top, and sniffed.

"What is this?" she asked suspiciously. "It smells like fruit."

"It tastes like fruit. It's made with it. That, and some plant extracts."

When she pursed her lips, he grabbed the flask, took a swig, and returned it to her hand.

"It's not illegal, if that's what you're worried about. It's called sundrops. It helps wake you up."

She stared at the flask for a few seconds more before finally taking a drink. Her tongue tapped loudly, reminding Dietrich of a hound who'd gotten something stuck in its mouth.

"Verdict?"

"It's good. Too good. I imagine I'd drink that all the time if I could."

"It's rather inexpensive in Sarabai. I could purchase you more, if you'd like."

"You promise it's not bad for the body?"

He chuckled. "No, princess. Don't worry. That perfect figure of yours won't be ruined."

She plopped down on her faux pillow again and, he noted, didn't hand the flask back.

"My query was in regard to organs. The heart, the liver, the lungs." She lay flat on her back, crossing one leg over the other. "It's tremendously helpful to know my *perfect figure* won't be altered, though."

He ignored the sarcasm in her voice. "Do you never indulge, then? No alcohol, no herbs?"

"I've had some wine and mead, no herbs. I don't like the lack of control."

"Ah." He grabbed a canteen of water. "That's not surprising in the slightest."

"Why?"

"You don't seem like someone who knows how to enjoy themselves."

She pulled down the arm she'd draped over her eyes and glared.

"I know how to enjoy myself."

"Oh? What do you consider fun?"

She opened her mouth to answer, quieted, then held up a finger.

"I like sparring."

"You're proving my point."

"What? Physical activity can't be enjoyable?"

"No," he said, stealing the flask of sundrops back. "That's not what I'm saying. I definitely agree that physical activity can be enjoyable. Just perhaps not the same . . . subgenre of physical activity that you deem exciting."

"Sparring is exciting," she said, cheeks reddening. "And I'm sure other subgenres are enjoyable as well. My defense still stands."

"It most certainly does not."

"Are you saying you don't enjoy fighting? You don't enjoy that feeling of someone underestimating you? Of dominating them?"

Dietrich grinned. "What's it like playing games with you I wonder. I'm sure you aren't upset *at all* when you lose. You probably say, 'Ah, well, it was nice just to be with everyone.'"

"Answer the question."

He dipped his head in submission. "I would be remiss not to admit that dominating another person is, indeed, enjoyable. However." He held up a finger. "I was not referring to enjoyment of those sorts. I meant relaxation. The pleasant warmth of drink, or the headiness of certain kinds of smoke. You aren't curious about that?"

"Nope."

"What calms you, then?"

"I don't know. My harp, I suppose. That always calmed me."

He stretched his legs, touched his toes, and rose.

"I stand corrected. Music is a fine means of relaxing. I still don't think you know how to let loose, but that's fine. I'll teach you."

He extended his hand to her. She made a face, saddened, apparently, at already having to leave the field, but she acquiesced, accepting his hand and standing.

They commented on how damp their clothes felt after sitting in the grass. For Dietrich, it was only in his trousers, but Gwenivere, having completely laid down, felt damp all over. She made to put her jacket on, but it was damp too, as was her scarf.

"Here," Dietrich offered, handing her his own jacket. "I'm quite warm now anyway."

She sighed. "I'm going to look like the stick that holds up a tent in this."

It was, indeed, enormous on her. Dietrich was about to tease her for it, but he was rather amused by how absurd it looked and, knowing she'd likely throw it back at him if he said anything, decided to keep quiet.

They ran through the notes he'd written regarding the directions to the Sanctuary. With how much people had avoided the Serpent's Breath, the path to it had long become overgrown, leaving nothing but more grass and flowers. As beautiful as the forest was, it wasn't particularly different the further in they went. Dietrich imagined that after a few hours, with how alluring the lights were and how captivating the trees must look at night, the forest would become quite easy to get lost in.

The Redeemers, then, had made nearly unnoticeable markers to help guide them. Sometimes it was a branch with a tiny brown ribbon tied to it, blending in with the rest of the tree. Other times, it was a scratch on a small boulder on the ground, or a flower that wasn't native to the forest poking out from among the other blooms.

Dietrich found each new marker they were looking for. He'd been worried Eren and the other tradesmen had lied to them, hoping he and Gwenivere would get lost in the forest and not be able to find their way out, but it seemed, with each new direction proven accurate, they'd been given good information after all.

That made him hopeful for the Serpent's Breath itself. According to Eren, the Redeemers had developed a spray and doused the caves with it every two weeks. It either completely eliminated the threat of the mushrooms' pollutants or diminished the effects to a point of tolerability.

Dietrich kept reminding Gwenivere of this the closer they got to the caves. She kept insisting she was fine and that the thought of taking a breath and vomiting up her intestines wasn't frightening in the slightest.

"Oh yes," he muttered, after she finished with the horrific picture she'd been painting. "You aren't scared at all."

He lowered his internal shield, nudging Seera through their bond.

You awake? he asked.

Unfortunately. Why?

Can you sense where I am?

Same answer.

I'm about to go into some caves. My reports say there should be cracks in the ceiling, big enough to let in light. If you're able to, can you try to follow us as we go through the caves? In case we get lost or need a quick escape, it could be helpful to have your eyes above.

Fine.

Could you also take note of any areas where the cracks are wide enough to either let people through, or lower goods down?

All right.

Thank you.

He didn't close the connection this time.

After another hour of walking, they finally found the cave entrance. They knew they were getting closer as purple and orange mushrooms slowly started replacing the flowers, but the suddenness of the cave's entrance surprised them both.

"I guess we're here," Rynara said quietly.

Dietrich put a hand on her shoulder, startling her, though the tension seeped away as he gently squeezed.

"I'll go in first," he said. "I'll walk until you can just barely see me, and then you can start walking. I'll call back to you if something isn't right. And Seera is on her way. She'll be above us the whole time. If something happens, and you need to get out, just run back, and she'll find you."

I didn't agree to that, Seera said. Dietrich couldn't see her, and he'd not sent the words through their bond, which meant she was already close enough to hear him.

You know you wouldn't just leave her, he said. *Stop pretending to be heartless.*

She made a point to huff through the bond but otherwise kept quiet.

"No," Gwenivere said. "No, we go in together. I'm fine, really. I'd rather be with you."

"You sure? You don't seem—"

"Really." She took the hand from her shoulder. "Dying doesn't scare me."

"Dying, maybe," he said. "Throwing up so much that blood starts—"

"Yes, yes! I know what I said. Can we go?"

"Yes. Let's."

As soon as they crossed into the cave, the air changed. No longer was it cool and open. There was a haziness to it, like a hot room that needed a window to open, though the space wasn't warm. It was more a humid feeling, a cloying, ever-present moisture. It made Dietrich nervous to breathe in, lest he fill his lungs with something toxic.

In truth, he was suddenly feeling afraid himself, but he didn't want Gwenivere to see his fear. One of them had to brave, and she was already trying so hard. The last thing he wanted to do was panic and crumble the stones of resolve she'd stacked.

The space was quite open, and the cracks above them did allow sunlight. The color wasn't quite right, though; rather than being warm, it somehow came through as more of a green-blue, and if he looked closely, he could see tiny flecks in the air where the light hit. He surmised the mushrooms here *had* released something: a thin veil of fog that'd distorted the sunlight's colors.

After the first turn in the cave, only fifty or so yards in, the ground beneath them became a small stream and the mushrooms catapulted in height. They were now as big as Gwenivere, some even as tall as Dietrich. There were the occasional trees or vines as well that were nothing but dark sticks hanging down from above. Dietrich guessed they were roots from trees on the surface, but he couldn't be sure.

They looked like tendrils, slowly reaching down to them.

He licked his lips and swallowed.

The cracks are small here, Seera said. *You might be able to slip very small items through, but so far, no person-sized gaps.*

Thank you, Dietrich answered. He shuddered as one of the mushrooms moved.

It only took two more enormous caverns before the mushrooms were the size of houses. Gwenivere gaped, and he found he was doing the same, the sight so disturbing and beautiful that he stopped thinking about being afraid.

There was a wrongness to the place, a sense of foreboding at seeing something that was supposed to be small so massive in size. Even still, the alienness of it all was strangely bewitching. If he didn't know better, Dietrich would think the pollutants were enchanting him.

The bottoms of the mushroom heads glowed. The colors were somewhere between orange and pink and purple, though the green tint to the sunlight never changed. It was as though someone had taken the whimsy of the forest outside and cast it through a portal until something sinister and menacing had taken shape.

Their footsteps made small splashing noises as they walked further in. Seera reported that the cracks still hadn't expanded, but that it did look as though there was a spot where people might deposit goods.

The trees up here have been cleared, she said. *And I see remnants of campfires. If I had to guess, I'd say contraband is slipped in at this spot. I imagine the two of you are close.*

Hearing that, Dietrich grabbed Gwenivere's hand, and took her out of the light. She didn't protest. He wasn't sure she even noticed.

If they were closing in on the Sanctuary, there might be people standing guard outside of it. Better they keep to the shadows and peer around corners.

After another half hour of walking, they finally found it.

There was no mistaking it. The cave, which had already been spacious, opened up into a sprawling, massive, city-like labyrinth. Stones reached from one side to the next, creating natural walkways covered in pink and yellow moss. A simple, circular structure had been erected in the center, and the mushrooms, which were not as close together here, but sparing, looked like sentries keeping watch over the Sanctuary's walls.

The whole thing was surreal. The Sanctuary seemed a distorted painting of a fortress in the woods or a small woodland city. The fact that it produced and distributed illegal goods made Dietrich want to tear it all down. Especially knowing those goods were passed through enslaved hands.

Frustratingly, he couldn't tear it down, even if he tried. If Seera attempted to burn her way through the top, or if the two of them both *called* earth and tried to make the place collapse in on itself, they'd kill all the people inside. And that was *if* he and Seera could even force the walls to fall.

If it were only Redeemers inside, Dietrich might consider the plan. With innocent people, taken from their families, kidnapped in the night, and forced into servitude?

He wouldn't risk their lives, even if it wiped out every Redeemer.

"We watch," Gwenivere whispered. "See if we spot anyone going in and out, or guarding the front."

Her fears seemed to evaporate. Give her something to be angry about and apparently her rage would take over.

Seera, what does it look like on your end? Dietrich asked.

The cracks are bigger here, she answered. *People might be able to slip through, but they'd need someone to lower them down by a rope. The drop is too far.*

Dietrich passed the information along to Gwenivere. She took it in with a nod, but her eyes were locked on the Sanctuary.

They sat for nearly an hour before they saw anyone come out. Dietrich instinctively put himself in front of Gwenivere, which he'd not realized he'd done until she swatted his side and moved in beside him.

"You lumbering giant!" she hissed. "I can't see anything when you get in front of me."

"Sorry."

The group of men, three in total, wore clothing no different than anyone else in Sarabai. They were speaking in Prianthian, and laughed about something, the sound bouncing off the cave walls. Eventually, after the cadence of their words indicated the conversation was done, they each went up different sides of the cave, spears in hand, and began crossing the stone walkways.

Guards, then. Either Gwenivere and her group would have to fight their way from the front, or they'd have to risk dropping down from above.

Neither option was great, and without knowing how many people there were and what sat inside, it was difficult to make any concrete decisions.

"We should leave," he whispered, grabbing her arm. "If they have a shipment scheduled to come, and they come through here, there's no way they don't see us."

Reluctantly, Gwenivere tore her eyes from the Sanctuary and nodded.

As soon as they'd returned to the forest, Dietrich put his hands on his knees, and took in a large gulp of air.

He'd noted immediately that the cave felt different, but it wasn't until he'd gone through it, grown accustomed to the strange sensation, and walked back out, that he realized how stale and heavy it'd felt. He'd heard that high elevation was more difficult on the lungs then sea level. He wondered if that's what this was like, though in this instance, he was feeling the difference all at once.

Standing upright, and rubbing his chest, he looked back at Gwenivere to make sure she wasn't hurt.

To his surprise, she didn't have her hands on her hips, or her knees. She'd sat down, back against a tree, and pulled off a boot.

"Are you injured?" he asked, walking over to her.

"I hurt it the other day." She gingerly pressed on her ankle. "It was fine earlier, but I think all the walking has worn it out a bit."

"May I?"

Dietrich crouched down to the ground in front of her, holding his hand out. She stared at him, unsure, but nodded.

He pulled off her stocking, then took her other leg and removed the boot and stocking from it too. It was obvious right away that one ankle was bigger than the other, and a light bit of yellow showed that bruising had formed.

Taking Gwenivere's scarf from her satchel, he *called* ice, similar to how he'd done for Zelhada, then wrapped the ankle. He carefully put her boot back on, making sure to tie the laces tight where they went from foot to leg, so as to limit her mobility left and right, but not up and down.

When he looked back at her, he was startled to find her eyes boring into him.

"Thank you," he said, unsure what her expression meant. "For letting me help you."

She blinked, though the intensity in her eyes didn't fade.

"I should be thanking you."

"Feel free, if you'd like." He grabbed her other boot and handed it over. "Here you are."

"Thank you."

She finally looked away.

Seera, Dietrich said, standing back up. *Our princess is hurt, it seems. Care to transport us back to the outskirts of the city?*

I'm not a horse, she said, though when he looked up, he saw her head poke out from behind the stones above the cave entrance. Her tail flicked behind her.

"Ryn," Dietrich said. "I believe you remember Seera."

The princess tensed as Seera slowly climbed down the rocks. She could've easily opened her wings and been down in seconds, but she seemed to relish the wide-eyed revery Gwenivere gave her.

The dragon was certainly one for grand entrances.

Awed, Gwenivere hurriedly finished tying her boot and stood. She stepped forward, then back, then halted, her eyes looking between Seera and Dietrich.

Seera walked up to them, lowering her head. Dietrich smiled, excited to have a moment where another person could see the dragon and not immediately associate her with death, or fear, or assassinations.

"How do you wish to be addressed?" Gwenivere asked. She looked Seera in the eye, turquoise meeting ice, then glanced at Dietrich, waiting for him to interpret.

He was so enthralled by the moment that he nearly forgot to relay his dragon's answer.

"Seera is fine," he said quickly. "If you wish for something more formal, 'O Great One,' apparently, is also acceptable."

The corners of Gwenivere's mouth twitched. She swallowed, still seeming uncertain, then dipped her head in a bow.

"May I approach you, Seera?"

Has she forgotten the Attack of Fiends? the dragon asked. *We've met before.*

She has certainly not *forgotten,* he answered. *She's trying to show you respect. Isn't that what you always want from everyone else? Stop being difficult.*

"You can approach," Dietrich said, not waiting for Seera's response.

Gwenivere finally walked forward without hesitation. Her breaths were loud and shallow, and when her hand reached up to Seera's neck, it was shaking.

"May I?" she asked, before letting her fingers touch Seera's quills. Dietrich was about to translate, but his dragon nodded.

Gwenivere beamed.

"They're softer than I expected," she whispered. "Almost like hair."

"They harden," Dietrich said. "They're almost like muscles she can flex. When she does, it makes it easier to hold. She can harden specific ones here." He gestured to her neck, where he usually held while flying. "While keeping these soft, so they don't pierce me through in flight."

To demonstrate his point, Seera flexed all but the quills Gwenivere held. She gasped, then laughed, and Seera let out a pleased purr.

Dietrich watched, transfixed. He'd never expected this moment. He'd never expected anything remotely *like* this moment.

After what he'd done in Sovereignty, he'd resigned himself to a life alone with Seera. He'd find Dorian's betrothed, deliver her the letters, then retreat back to the mountains, where Zoran's old dwelling had been, and he'd live his life out in solitude.

He'd have Seera to keep him company, and she'd have him, but otherwise, he'd keep himself not only exiled from his home, but from the rest of humankind as well.

Seera, who'd been excited to return home, had abruptly changed her mind.

I don't want to spend my days with you if you're only going to cry and mope all the time. You're far more tolerable when you have something to set your mind on.

He knew what she'd really been saying.

You're already letting yourself die. I don't want to be the reason you forget to live.

Now he was here, watching the two most irritable beings he'd ever met come together. He swallowed, forcing down the sudden welling of tears threatening to break through.

Tell her thank you, Seera said, *for saving you after the attack.*

Dietrich relayed the words.

"Thank you for saving my home," Gwenivere answered. Her voice was soft, and soothing, and Seera curled her neck and opened her wing, enveloping Gwenivere in a hug.

"You can hold her back," Dietrich said, pointing to her neck. "Just be careful with your hair. It might get caught in her quills."

Gwenivere nodded, her arms wrapping around the dragon.

This is very sweet, Dietrich said. *Is there a reason you're so withholding when it comes to your affection with me?*

You're far more annoying. And I don't think she's been able to do this with anyone for a long time.

Dietrich took in Seera's words, noting the tightness of Gwenivere's hold. As she let go, and Seera opened up again, he walked over, placing his own hands on the scales of her neck and chest.

"She doesn't like the cold," he said. "If you *call* a bit of fire, and rub it into her scales, it helps."

Nodding, Gwenivere immediately *called* fire and began following Dietrich's hands.

"I imagine this is relaxing," she said, smiling up at Seera.

"She certainly enjoys it, especially right before she sleeps, or before—"

"No." Gwenivere's voice was quiet as she met his eyes. "For you. What you said earlier, about finding things enjoyable." She smiled. "I think I would very much enjoy doing this."

"You're doing it now."

"I know. It just doesn't seem real."

"No. It doesn't."

Seera dipped her head, shooing them apart.

Speaking of sleep, she said, *I'd really like to return to it, so if you both could hurry along, I'd like to get this over with.*

"You didn't do anything wrong," Dietrich said, dipping his head under Seera's. "She's just responsibly reminding us that we should head back before it gets dark."

"Oh, yes. Thank you, Seera."

Gwenivere bowed her head, then stepped back as Dietrich climbed onto Seera's back.

Do you mind? he said to her, nudging her with his knees. *She's not used to getting on and off, and if you haven't noticed, she's not exactly tall enough to hop up.*

Wordlessly, Seera bent her legs. Dietrich reached down, offering Gwenivere his hand.

"Behind me, or in front?"

"Which do you think?"

"Seera won't let you fall, but I'd feel better if you were in front."

"Front it is."

She grabbed the hand he offered and let out a small yelp as he lifted her completely up. Seera didn't have a saddle, and she hated using the quills on her sides as stirrups. Better to keep the princess on his dragon's good side for as long as possible.

"Any quills," he instructed.

Gwenivere leaned forward and grabbed on. He expected her grip to be tight, but she held on gently, as though she didn't want to hurt Seera.

He thought to tell her to tighten her hold, but decided that unlike their flight escaping the Behemoth, Seera likely wouldn't be plummeting them to near death every few seconds.

Leaning forward, and trying not to intrude too strongly into Gwenivere's space, Dietrich grabbed the quills on either side of where she held, tightened the muscles in his legs, and took a breath.

Seera opened her wings and flew. It was always surprising how little start she needed to launch herself into the air. Gwenivere's grip immediately tightened, as Dietrich had expected it would, but he hadn't expected her to laugh too. She leaned forward, as though he wasn't there, and it was she and Seera alone.

The sun was high in the sky now and beaming down on them. The air above the treetops was crisp, and cold, and even with Seera's languid speed, it still bit at his skin. He had to squint to keep it from his eyes; it and Gwenivere's hair, which whipped wildly from her place in front of him.

A new beginning? Seera asked, pressing into Dietrich's mind. He'd not said the thought to her, but the memory of that morning must have risen up, unbidden.

Thanks to you, he said, rubbing his hand on her neck.

Not just me, Seera replied, and though she didn't say more, he could sense the smile in her words.

CHAPTER FIFTY-ONE

RYNARA

The flight was over far too quickly.

Despite having ridden with Seera before, this felt like the first time. During the attack, Rynara's mind had been too lost in the chaos, too consumed by the fear of the Behemoth, and her city, and whether her father and brother were safe. She'd hardly had time to appreciate the feel of the massive being guiding her on the wind. She'd not been able to take in the peace that came from being among the clouds and the birds and the beasts of the sky.

It was liberation and joy. It was frightening and exhilarating.

It was dangerous, and foolhardy, and she'd never felt safer in her life.

"Thank you," she said to Seera, as Dietrich helped her from her back. She slid down, grimacing as she landed on her sore ankle. Dietrich kept his arms around her, holding her, it appeared, until she was confident she could stand.

"Thank you to as you as well," she said, looking up at him.

He still hadn't let go. She held her breath, unsure how to catch it after the excitement of flight.

"Can you walk?"

"Yes, thank you."

"You're sure?"

She smiled, wanting to show him she could, but not wanting to release the security that came from his grip.

"Yes," she said, nodding. She brushed her hair from her eyes, certain the strands were sticking up wildly. "I'm sure."

Dietrich seemed to realize he'd not released her, then did so quickly before patting Seera one last time.

"As she said," he told the dragon. "Thank you."

Rynara didn't know what passed between them, but he saw his face twist into something akin to exasperation. Seera turned her crystal eyes to her, nudging her a bit forcefully, then turned, opened her wings, and retreated back toward the mountains.

"What did she say to you?" Rynara asked, patting down her hair.

Dietrich seemed to find anywhere to glance but her.

"Nothing really."

"Is it tiresome, having it be two people?"

He checked the straps of their satchels, then pulled out two canteens of water, handing her one.

"Can't say."

Rynara sipped her water. She was sad to step forward and remember that this—this boring, slow, tiresome path—was how she'd have to usually see the world.

They were still about an hour away from the outskirts of the city. Dietrich had thought it wise to keep Seera away from where people were, especially with the printings still running stories about him and the dragon at the coliseum. Rynara agreed, though it hadn't really been up to her. When it came to the dragon, she was well aware that whatever Dietrich decided was best.

The wrapping around her ankle was stiff, but snug. There was still an ache present, but it felt more like fatigue rather than pain. It made walking tolerable, but not pleasant.

"Where to?" Dietrich asked, as they came up to a forked path.

"I need to meet with Teniv tonight. She's the woman you. . . ." She tapped on her neck. "That's not until later, though. I think we should return to the tradesmen first. They've been on the top of the clock tower since last night. Now that we've confirmed the information they've given us, it might be best to turn them over to the enforcers."

Dietrich pointed to the path with a sign: CLOCK TOWER THIS WAY.

"What do you think? Is it this one?"

She smiled, but the lack of sleep was catching up to her, and she didn't have the energy to play along.

While it wasn't hot, it was certainly warmer than it'd been before sunrise that morning. They both stopped to drink all but one of the waters left, then passed the flask of sundrops back and forth. Rynara offered Dietrich some of the salted seeds she'd brought, but he politely declined.

Exhaustion seemed to be catching up to both of them. Neither spoke most of the way back to the city. Occasionally Rynara winced if she stepped wrong, and Dietrich would place a worried hand out and ask if she was all right, but otherwise, their return to Sarabai was quiet and uneventful.

That changed quickly when they reached the Tower's Shadow.

Another crowd had formed. At first Rynara feared the Redeemers were holding another execution. She couldn't imagine they'd risk that after what'd happened a few days before, and none of her Hawks had caught wind of any such plans. Plus, as part of their jubilation, the people of Sarabai had torn the gallows down and burned the wood. The Redeemers would've needed to rebuild the structure, hire or bring in more of their followers, and attempt to combat the fighting spirit that'd been reignited in the city.

But no, the crowd didn't seem angry this time. They seemed manic, almost, but not angry.

They were loud and boisterous and excited. They were like the rapids of a river. The hooves of a herd.

Rynara cursed her short height, wishing she could see what was happening. The maelstrom of sound was giving her a headache. The press of so many bodies made her dizzy.

People let out a collective cheer.

She turned to Dietrich, trying to determine if he'd seen what'd happened.

His body went completely still.

"What?" she asked. "What's going on?"

He snapped to attention, grabbing her arm and yanking her aside. A part of her was glad to escape the heat of the crowd. The other part was furious.

"What are you doing?" she hissed. Even with the distance he'd put between them and the people nearby, she still kept her voice low, not wanting to draw attention.

"You don't want to see what's down there."

She wriggled her arm free.

"I need to know."

She softened, noting the horror in his eyes. For him to look the way he did, pale, sweaty, shocked, she knew something had gone terribly wrong.

"The tradesmen," he said. "They were found. The barricade we put on the doors must've been broken through. People are ... people are killing them."

Rynara shoved her way back into the crowd. Dietrich followed close behind, his larger frame cutting through more easily.

There were curses directed at them, a couple of people spitting, but most seemed too distracted to care for long. Rynara managed to reach the edge of the walkway they were on, which looked over the Tower's Shadow, not quite as high as the clock tower itself, but enough to grant her a view of what lay beneath.

A few other people pressed against her, one stepping on her foot, another smashing her hand against the walkway's railing. Cursing, Rynara spun around, *called* air, and, with a gust of wind, pushed them away.

"Stand back!"

Dietrich, seeming to sense the wrath of the crowd, added, "It's the Phoenix!"

The anger immediately shifted, swapped by quiet awe. A few people whispered. A few apologized.

Taking advantage of the short calm, Rynara turned back to the roof's edge, peering at the scene below.

Where the executions were meant to take place now stood hundreds of people. The fearful quiet they'd possessed only a few days before was replaced by a frenzied, hyper, gleeful fury.

Rynara had never seen anything like it. They were a mob motivated by hate and revenge, yet hungry, desperate even, so collectively lustful for blood it seemed an almost primal, sensual thing.

They'd managed to cluster together tightly enough to allow for an open space to form between them, uneven and circular.

Within in it lay two bodies.

The crowd was cheering.

Then they all looked up.

Up, up, up, to the place she'd jumped from before. To the place where now, a group of people stood, shouting to the crowd below, "This one too?"

They held Eren, the third tradesman, on the edge of the clock tower. Rynara couldn't hear him, but even from a distance, she knew his face was twisted with tears.

She remembered Dietrich holding Eren over the edge. She remembered what he'd said.

After everything you've done, I think if anyone saw you up here, screaming in such a fashion, and they realized who you were, I'm rather certain they'd encourage me to let go.

They didn't just encourage. They begged. Screamed. Shook. Jumped. They began chanting, fists pounding in the air.

It took a moment for Rynara to decipher the chant.

Drop him.

"Don't watch," Dietrich whispered, suddenly there. He stood slightly behind her, a shield between her and the eager crowd around them. Even after her orders, even after the respect they'd granted her, the people around her were closing in, ravenous for the violence they were about to see.

Rynara wanted to stop them. She wanted to press everyone back again, then leap from the balcony and demand everyone cease their madness. She wanted to snap everyone out of it, put the dead tradesmen back together, keep Eren from being dropped. There was no love in her heart for the man, but he didn't deserve this. What of the mother he'd been trying to help? Was she in the crowd? Who would care for her, once her son hit the ground?

She could do none of that. If she put herself in the middle of that mob, and made any attempts to change their minds, they'd tear her apart.

There was no stopping what was about to happen. She could only bear witness to what her lawlessness wrought.

They let him go. No one stopped his descent.

His body hit with a sickening crack.

He'd still been bound when they'd dropped him. His neck snapped at a terrible angle. His head burst open.

Rynara flinched.

The mob erupted.

With Eren being the last of the three tradesmen dead, bodies shoved forward, filling the circle they'd formed.

Rynara couldn't imagine what they could possibly want from the bodies or what there was left to do with them. The men were already dead.

The crowd should've had enough.

They'll burn them, likely, she thought, trying to keep herself calm. It was common during wartime to burn the bodies of enemies. Burning was believed to force *auroras* from the bodies of the dead too quickly. It was like the soul itself was being ripped from its host. No one could know for certain if that was true or if it was painful, but there was something about the way *auroras* almost screamed when forced from the body before the three-day mark that left the theory relatively uncontested.

Expecting the burning made Rynara feel as though she were one of Xenith's generals, having delivered the enemy to the people they'd harmed. She should be able stand tall, knowing she held a place among those who'd come before her, the mighty soldiers who lived in many a painting across her palace's walls.

She wished the pride she was supposed to feel would sink in. She wished she could quell the urge to vomit and shout and cry.

It was not a fire that was built, though.

Instead of flames emerging from the plaza, the bloodied

hands of Sarabaens lifted. There was more yelling. Laughter, animated and pleased, bubbled up from the crowd.

Rynara stumbled, realizing what they'd done. Dietrich was there, one hand pressed firmly to her back, the other holding the underside of her arm. She wordlessly thanked him, almost imperceptibly dipping her chin, then straightened, leaning on the walkway's railing.

The mob might yet still burn the bodies. Maybe. For now, they held up the heads of the tradesmen, arms covered in blood, before passing and tossing them around.

"I need to tell the others," she said. "About this, and . . . and everything else we learned today. Will you walk with me, until we're away from here?"

"Of course."

It took some time before Rynara felt she could properly breathe again. There were more direct routes to the warehouse for her meeting with Teniv, Luthier, and the other Hawks, but she wanted some time to walk, blisters and worn ankle forgotten, before she saw them.

If she met with them too soon after what she'd just seen, she feared they'd see the mortification in her eyes—the shock

—and be more concerned with doting on her or reassuring her it wasn't her fault than they would be on the matters at hand.

Walking slowly, and taking in the fresh air, Rynara and Dietrich made their way through quieter parts of the city. A number of times, enforcers passed opposite them, weapons at the ready, heavily armored bodies trudging along with urgency. She wondered how many of them didn't care about what they would see. Would they join in the revelry? The ecstasy of bloodshed? For those who didn't, were they ready for what they were about to find? How much worse would the situation be, by the time they got there?

Would anyone even be able to recognize the bodies?

Rynara kept on. One foot in front of the other.

Dietrich followed behind.

"I'm not sure you should attend this meeting," she said. "I've not yet explained to the others about you, and I'd rather the meeting primarily be centered on what we discovered about the Sanctuary."

"I was thinking the same thing. Do you want me to wait outside?"

She shook her head. "No, that won't be necessary. I don't want them thinking I need a bodyguard or a spy protecting me from them, if they happen to spot you. It won't go far in the way of trust. You can go back to the Tired Cat, if you'd like. Or whatever else you feel up to. I don't much care."

She waved her hand flippantly, stopped, then decided she very, very much needed to sit down. The area around them was homes on one side and a small field of grass and trees on the other. She chose the closest tree to where they stood and sauntered over to it, plopping herself down and folding her legs beneath her. Dietrich did the same, one shoulder of his touching one of hers, one leg bent, the other outstretched.

"I should've moved them," he said. "I should've found a different place to keep them."

"Don't," she said, pinching the bridge of her nose. "I mean, yes, we should've found someplace else to put them, or turned them over to the enforcers—something else. But we didn't. And note I'm saying *we*. I wasn't thinking straight myself last night. I was too eager about the information for the Sanctuary."

"The enforcers killed the others," he said. "I looked into it last night, after we parted ways. They did it with less fanfare, but I'm not sure you'd have felt much better if we'd turned the tradesmen over too."

He blew air from his cheeks. Noisily. It seemed almost comical. It was far from funny, but she oddly felt the urge to laugh.

"Do you think it was the Redeemers who actually killed them?" she asked. "Do you think they were trying to cover their tracks?"

"I don't know. I'm not sure it really matters."

"I suppose it doesn't."

They sat for a while. Dietrich gave her more sundrops, noting that she'd need the energy for the meeting coming up. She insisted they drink more water, as they'd likely not packed enough for how long the trek to the Sanctuary had been, and it was important they stay hydrated. *Water helps with fatigue too*, she thought, though it really wasn't worth saying.

Silence was all they seemed capable of, for a time, as they quietly passed the canteens of water and sundrops back and forth.

When they'd finished both, they shared some unspoken agreement that it was necessary they get back to their day. She told him she'd relay any important information discussed at the meeting back at the Tired Cat, and he told her he'd go get some sleep.

"Some horrible woman made me wake up very early," he said, returning her satchel. "I want to make sure I'm plenty awake when she visits me tonight."

She felt a bit empty, then, as they went down their separate paths. His presence had been something solid for her to cling to, and now that he was walking away, the reality of what she'd seen started to settle.

The sense of wrongness, of loneliness, of having to process her thoughts alone, made her suddenly very anxious to be near people.

More than anything, or anyone, she wanted to see Luthier. She wanted to be close to him, if only to borrow some of his steady calm, that resounding, stoic strength he always seemed to possess. She was glad, for his sake, after hearing the crack of Eren's body on the ground, after seeing the horrible angle of his neck, that she hadn't followed through on the temptation to fling herself off a roof only a short time ago.

She couldn't begin to fathom what it would've done to her knight, if it'd been her body on the ground and his eyes watching it happen.

I need to apologize to him, she reminded herself. *I need him to know how much he means to me.*

Concentrating on that, and forcing out, or down, or away, all the haunting thoughts now plaguing her, Rynara made her way to Teniv's old warehouse, eager to refocus her mind on the task ahead of them and not on all the ways she'd played a part in what she'd seen.

CHAPTER FIFTY-TWO
RYNARA

The warehouse was used for storage.

With how many people had started moving to Sarabai the last few years, many a wealthy homeowner in the Dividing Wall, Voradeen, or Riverdee traveled to the clock city and found their coin only afforded them a small apartment. They thought it was worth it for a variety of reasons—the temperate climate, the innovation, the opportunities—but often the things they'd brought with them on carts and wagons couldn't fit in their new dwellings.

Knowing how sentimental people could be, Teniv had bought several warehouses in Sarabai just before the city's population had boomed. For a fee every season, people could store whatever things they didn't have room for in their homes but loved too much to sell. Visiting hours to see the items were only on some days of the week. The rest of the time, employers cleared out belongings from those who hadn't paid, cleaned the space, checked for rats or other vermin. Or, as was the case today, they did nothing.

On nothing days, Teniv set up a mismatched array of

lounge chairs, rocking chairs, sofas, and whatever else she thought looked comfortable, and she made a colorful and comfortable place for the Hawks to meet.

Rynara came through a different entrance than everyone else. She kept to the back, her body hidden by an old armoire and a few bookcases.

She wasn't ready to be seen just yet. The day had been a whirlwind of information and feelings, in some ways a reminder of all she strove for. In others, it was an addition to the horrors that haunted her at night.

I don't think you should keep doing this.

Luthier's words, only a few days before.

You've brought a new beginning to a lot of people.

Dietrich's words, mere hours before.

She listened to the chatter of Hawks as they poured themselves some of Teniv's best wine. Given her many connections, and the many taverns she owned, the older woman often found herself in possession of beverages most people wouldn't be able to afford in their entire lives. One of the Hawks, a Sadiyan girl of indiscernible age named Sasha, joked that the wine was the main reason she joined.

Already, they were discussing the news of what'd happened to the tradesmen. The crackling of conversation carried to Rynara's hiding place revealed that while the Hawks weren't sure of the specifics, a few of them had been in the mob when it'd happened.

Rynara slunk down, pulling her legs to her chest. She wanted silence. That, or she wanted meaningless noise. Music, maybe. Or a cheery fire in a hearth. Though it might unsettle her nerves, she'd even take the rumble of a distant storm.

Luthier's right, she thought, wrapping her arms around her legs and resting her head against her knees. *I can't keep doing this.*

No. That's not what he'd told her.

He'd told her she *shouldn't* keep doing this.

Her knight believed her capable of whatever she put her mind to. He'd proven countless times over her life that he followed her not because she was his charge, but because he thought her worthy of his devotion.

He'd also proven he loved her as a parent did their child. It was a gift, to have someone be her everything, as he was. It was also a curse, for him at least, to have the various roles he filled constantly warring inside him.

Gwen?

She looked up.

No one was there.

The voice hadn't been spoken, she realized. Not now, at least. It was a memory, one where she'd been smaller than her current size, with less muscles on her frame, and her hair red.

Gwen, was your father . . . unsettled again?

She'd been fourteen. Too old to hide in her wardrobe.

The dresses had made her feel safe, though. Some of them had been her mother's.

I tried to come with him, she'd explained. *He found me pretending to be one of the squires.*

She'd not cried at the question or her answer. She'd only closed her hand over the finger marks on arm.

I see, Garron had said. He'd not whispered, but he'd crouched down until he was level with her. He spoke gently. *He's left now. He'll be in Mesidia for at least a few weeks, and I know there are some sword stances he didn't want you learning, but if you don't tell, I won't either.*

He'd offered her a hand and smiled.

Rynara pulled herself from the memory. She wasn't surrounded by extravagant gowns; she was shoved between dusty shelves and old furniture. She wasn't about to spar with her knight. The warehouse wasn't her castle.

Standing, and brushing off her pant legs, Rynara became the Phoenix, slipped on her red cloak, and walked over to her Hawks.

"Is everyone accounted for?" she asked. A few of them startled, not realizing there was another entrance. To them, she'd materialized from thin air.

"All here," Teniv said.

"Good." Rynara nodded to the Hawks. Besides Teniv, Luthier, Sasha, and herself, there were sixteen additional people who Rynara had welcomed into her trusted circle. None of them besides Teniv and Luthier knew her true name, but the rest were allowed access to plans and information, they were given more coin than the other followers, and while most of them had at least a proficient level of skill for fighting, they were all willing to accept training from Teniv and Luthier.

Many of them were in the warehouse, but others had stayed behind in the towns and villages she'd liberated. They ensured the enforcers or city watch or whoever else was given authority stayed far removed from the Redeemers' hold.

Some cities, especially those with connections to nobility or wealthy merchant houses, couldn't be entirely purified. In those instances, the Hawks did everything they could to keep illegal contraband away, thus eliminating the potential for influence.

If they couldn't get to the people, they could get to the goods.

The meeting started with the Hawks seated before Rynara now updating her on what information they'd received from their contacts in the other towns. Each of them was responsible for maintaining contact with several of their brethren. They reported back any immediate emergencies, of which there were none, blessedly, and juxtaposed what they were hearing from their contacts against what gossip was traveling through.

It was important to Rynara that they compared facts against rumors. The truth meant nothing if the perception among the masses reigned supreme.

Rynara knew that from personal experience.

"Riverdee still seems to be the largest supplier of slave labor," Sasha said, moving from domestic to international connections. Though Rynara had yet to move her influence outside of Xenith, she understood logically that the Redeemers cared little for borders.

"Once we find the Sanctuary," Sasha continued, "I imagine the Redeemers will operate primarily from there. Sources indicate that the entire capital city watch is corrupted. The only reason—from what I can tell, at least—they haven't made a full exodus from Sarabai to there is because the Sanctuary dates back to before the trade ban. They'd already set themselves up here. If we find the Sanctuary and liberate it, we'll likely eradicate their hand in Xenith, but a hand in Riverdee could be disastrous."

"Agreed," Teniv said. "Riverdee has long been an ally to all, enemy to none. Its access to the ocean, its border with a handful of countries, and it being the main source of Evean goods has made it off limits for conquering. Any one country taking it over would turn every other country against it. Unofficially controlling it, though, at least through its trade, would mean the Redeemers would regulate the lifeblood of the continent."

"They'd become wealthier than they already are," Luthier added. "Once they have wealth comparable to kings, other countries won't bother trying to eradicate them."

Sasha nodded. "And let's not forget their main message.

They've preached to Prianthia and Sadie for over a decade at this point that the West is evil. To use your metaphor, Teniv, if they become the continent's lifeblood, then they could easily poison it. Trust me." She pointed to her green eyes. "For most of my life I've heard how much they hate you."

"Fear naught!" Antigone said. She was a short Xen woman, with more freckles than seemed possible, and auburn hair that wasn't quite red or brown. She was a lovely person, though her constant happiness was something Rynara found draining.

"I bring news from Riverdee," Antigone continued. "It would seem they have their own version of you, Phoenix."

She stood from a velvet chair and passed out printings to each of the Hawks. She gave Rynara one last. Not intentionally; she wasn't trying to make any kind of statement. She just often forgot, having been raised in a family with eleven children, that sometimes there was a hierarchy to things.

Rynara thanked her for the printing, glancing through it.

"An Evean?" she said, surprised. "They don't usually get involved in our politics."

"They've claimed she's the same person who led the Attack of Fiends in Riverdee," Antigone said. "Though others have come forward and claimed she helped them during and after a recent storm. A few even said they saw her helping people *during* the attack."

"She's been captured, though," Teniv said. "Does she have any followers? Any allies? She can't possibly be trying to eradicate the Redeemers on her own. They'll execute her immediately."

"The Redeemers have always had an undercurrent of religious fanaticism in their messaging," Sasha said. "The printing here says X'odia—that's the woman's name—willingly turned herself in. She was quoted saying, 'I am innocent in the eyes of the Creator, and soon, in the eyes of men. You will see that it's not you, Navar, that the Light blesses but me and all others who stand against darkness.'"

"That doesn't mean anything," Teniv said, disappointed. She tossed the printing on a nearby table and crossed her arms.

"It means everything," Sasha countered. "If she manages to win the favor of Riverdians, *and* she undercuts the faith people have placed in the Redeemers, she'll dismantle everything they've built there. It will be her word against theirs."

"Enough," Rynara said, holding her hand up. "We'll keep our eyes open to this situation, but there's no reason to argue over its merits so long as it's in a stalemate. If this X'odia woman does manage to rise up against the Redeemers, we'll make attempts to contact her and bring her to our side. If not, it's a moot point.

"Those of you assigned to Eastern information. Have there been any recent developments?"

Gregor, a burly Prianthian man, handed her a recent Xen printing. He didn't speak much, which had concerned Rynara initially, but then she'd recalled how little Luthier spoke, and her suspicions toward him softened. He'd actually become one of her favorite Hawks because of how little he irritated her and how dedicated he was to their cause.

"Anastasia's soldiers, who've been stationed outside of Sovereignty." He'd only brought the one printing, unlike Antigone. "King Abaddon has still not woken from his coma. Ambassador Dorian has made the decision to allow the soldiers into Sovereignty while the king remains inactive."

He returned to where he'd been standing beside Luthier and nodded that he was done speaking.

Dietrich . . . Rynara thought, gripping the printing tight. All of Dietrich's work to shift the blame to himself, and it seemed the Treaty of Five still wasn't doing anything to lift the ban and discourage the Prianthians from moving in.

I'll have to tell him of this tonight, she decided, stuffing the printing into her pocket. She gave a curt nod to Gregor, who dipped his head in acknowledgment. That was usually the extent of his exchanges.

"I will of course need to be kept abreast of this," she said, trying to sound unmoved. She didn't usually react to Eastern politics, but now, with what she knew, she found herself impassioned.

She didn't wish to show that though. The time wasn't right to reveal Dietrich Haroldson had become their ally, and her sudden concern with the East—outside of its connections to Redeemers—would be out of character.

"The Sanctuary was brought up earlier," she said, resisting the urge to bite her lip. "I'm sure many of you are aware of what happened to the tradesmen, but if not, a quick summary: After the execution, the three men who Sasha had discovered knew the Sanctuary's location escaped. Last night, I and another new member of our group"—she looked to Teniv as if to say, *See, the dangerous one proved helpful*—"questioned them. The man had captured them in an effort to prove his loyalty to our cause, and the two of us were able to get the information from them that we've been wanting."

The Hawks let out a collective gasp. The ones on benches nudged one another while the ones in large chairs sat up, trying to make eye contact with whomever was closest.

Teniv gave Rynara a playful punch, and Gregor gave another dip of his head.

Luthier, stoic as always, only looked on with furrowed brow.

"You celebrate too soon," she went on. "There is good and bad news to accompany this.

"The bad, as many of you were discussing earlier, is that the tradesmen were killed. I and our new connection had thought it best to barricade the clock tower's rooftop door and leave the men there until we'd confirmed whether their information was true. We intended to hand them over to the enforcers after we did so, but unfortunately, they were found and killed."

She swallowed, forcing down the sound of Eren's body hitting the ground.

"The good news, however, is that the information they gave us was sound. Earlier today, I traveled to the Sanctuary, and can confirm that we've found it."

The Hawks reacted. Rynara smiled, though it felt wrong to do so.

Some of them have had friends who've been taken to the Sanctuary, she thought. *Family, even. For them, this is it. This is the final battle of the war. If we take the Sanctuary, this plague in our country will be gone.*

She licked her lips, allowing the Hawks their revelry.

Teniv walked over to her, leaning down and whispering in her ear, "You've done well, Ryn."

They were simple words, but her guilt lessened.

She looked to Luthier. Beneath his beard, she saw him smile.

"You've got your good news," she said. She crossed her arms, hiding that her hands were shaking, and forced her shoulders back. "Now let's discuss the Sanctuary itself."

After all the Hawks but Luthier had left, Rynara finally took a seat.

They'd discussed different routes of entry and how they might destroy the building itself. Fire wasn't entirely out of the question, but it was a risk, given all the pollutants in the Cave of Death and Dreams. They didn't know how the flames would react, and it might result in more harm than good if they went about it unprepared.

Infiltration was an option, but from what they could tell, the Redeemers mostly kidnapped Westerners, ruling out a lot of the Hawks. Teniv, Rynara, and Luthier were options, but everyone agreed Rynara shouldn't be the one to go in. Teniv had too many connections, so, not knowing how close Rynara and Luthier actually were, Luthier remained an option.

She'd not liked that plan, but for now, it was only one of many options. First, she thought it important that more of the Hawks saw the caves for themselves. Maybe one of them would see something she and Dietrich hadn't.

"Hello," she said, as Luthier walked over. He took a seat on the now vacant bench several of the Hawks had been sitting on before.

"Hello," he said.

She coughed, then folded her hands in her lap.

"I'm sorry," she said. "For snapping at you."

His mouth quirked.

"For all the times, or...."

She laughed. Some of the tension she'd been holding slipped away.

"Sure, all," she said. "But more specifically, for the other day. I know you only want what's best for me. I know you want me to be safe. I want the same for you. If anything, between the two of us, you deserve to live out the rest of your life in peace. You already fought in the War of Fire. You didn't just fight—you became the most respected and renowned soldier in Xenith."

She'd opened her hands wide, as though the gesture could encapsulate just how grand of a title that was.

"Then you spent the rest of your life serving my family. You've been the most loyal knight I could've ever asked for. Now you have a chance to finally rest. If I asked you to stop, would you?"

He said no before she'd finished the question.

"Well," she continued. "That's how I feel too. I don't want to stop."

Luthier abandoned his rigid, perfect posture and leaned forward, elbows resting on his knees, hands laced together.

"Do you know that I held you before you father did?"

Rynara started at the question. She shook her head.

"He was away. For good reason—he was securing a trade deal that resulted in a great amount of work opportunities for Xens, but that's beside the point."

He cleared his throat.

"You remember I was your mother's knight, before yours, yes? I was there when she had you. After she held you, she wished to rest, and the midwives asked me if I could hold you while Rose slept. They said the skin-to-skin contact would be good for you.

"I'd never held an infant, let alone the heir to a country. I'd held baby animals, but that's not the same. I told them I was afraid I'd drop you."

Rynara smiled, curling her legs up in the chair. "I imagine I screamed quite loudly. And squirmed a lot."

"You did," he admitted. "I'm not sure Rose actually wanted rest; I think she just needed to build up the energy to deal with you. Before she fell asleep, she told me to stop being stupid, and that I was your knight, now, not hers, and that it was my responsibility to keep you safe. In that moment, keeping you safe meant letting her sleep, and holding you against my chest.

"You were very fat. Everyone ironically said you'd be tall, like your father. You made a lot of noise, and you were very pink, and all the midwives said you were beautiful and had that beautiful newborn smell, but I thought you looked and smelled odd."

"That's nice, Garron. Thank you."

"And then they told me to take off my shirt—which was very embarrassing for me, as I was very shy then—"

"Only then?"

"Hush. I was very shy then, and Rose said, 'Garron, you just saw urine, shit, and a baby come out of me, and you want to fuss over a bunch of women seeing your chest?' I'd never heard her curse before, so evidently having you impacted that.

"Anyway, I finally—although very reluctantly—took off my shirt, sat down in the chair at your mother's side, and let them hand you to me. They finished cleaning Rose up, and she went to sleep, and they left, and then it was just me and you. And even knowing you weren't mine, once you stopped crying and looked up at me, all I could think was, Light . . . how stupid I've been —to think I knew what love was."

Rynara nodded, then looked away. What was there to say, or what expression could you give, to convey an understanding that you were someone else's whole world?

"That's what you've given me," he said. "That's a gift every child gives their parent. What I give you, in return, is given freely. There's no trade or exchange that matches that."

"What you give me is *everything*," she said, annoyed when her voice came out choked. She gritted her teeth, pushing her tears down. Her chest ached from the effort.

"I know it was hard for you," she continued. "When my father . . . got angry. I know you felt like you'd failed me, but you didn't. You've always been my protector. But if you don't feel like you can do this anymore, if it's too difficult to watch me put myself in danger, that's all right too. I don't want you to go, but at some point . . . at some point every parent has to let their child live their life. I hope you'll stay in mine, but if it's too hard, I'll understand."

"I'm your knight," he said. "I will always be at your side."

"Are you sure?"

He smiled. It was a simple gesture but filled with a warmth that made Rynara feel like a child again.

"I'm sure."

CHAPTER FIFTY-THREE
RYNARA

Back at the Tired Cat, Rynara rapped on Dietrich's door. Unsurprisingly, she heard no stirring at all. Generally, there was a bustle of noise or a calling out that the person would be right there. Dietrich seemed to suddenly materialize before her, like an *aurora* being *called* into existence.

He smiled when he saw it was her.

"Here to relay the meeting's notes to me?" He stepped aside to let her in. If he noticed how stiff her shoulders were or the grim set of her mouth, he was doing a fine job ignoring it.

She mumbled something in reply. Glancing around the room, she saw the design and furniture were nearly identical to her own across the hall, though Dietrich's number of *touched* blades was much higher than her own, and the contents of whatever filled the vials beneath the window of the western wall were far more interesting—and likely deadly—than anything in her room. She walked over to them, bending to squint at the rainbow of concoctions. With the setting sun coming through the window, each vial was cast in a yellow glow, mixing with the already vibrant greens and blues and reds.

As much as she still felt a fool for agreeing to trust Dietrich, she was glad that, with what were likely extremely lethal poisons sitting haphazardly in his sleeping chambers, he had chosen a path that aligned with hers.

"You probably don't need telling," he said. "But it would be best if you didn't touch any. Especially the green one."

"Are these what you use for the needles?"

"Ah, no. Here, let's go through them." He crossed the room and joined her by the window. With long, gloved fingers, he delicately put a stopper over the top of a vial, lifted it from its holder, then held it up. "A drop of this will cause sweating and twitching. You could recover from it, but I'd advise caution when handling it.

"The exciting part is when it's no longer in liquid form. If turned into a gas, it can cause someone to lose consciousness, become paralyzed, fail to breathe . . ." He was staring at the liquid, the color a few shades away from his eyes, before suddenly looking back at her, clearing his throat, and putting the vial back.

"It's quite deadly, is the point."

"Oh really? I hadn't gotten that."

He laughed, but it was a strange, almost tittering sound. She stared at him, brows furrowed, trying to determine what had him behaving so oddly. Perhaps he was tired, and the fatigue was making him manic.

"I don't get to talk about this much," he said, noting her stare. "I used to be a fiend hunter. I'd bring certain parts back to Abaddon, and the two of us would try and come up with new cures together. He was usually the one to make the helpful discoveries. I usually had fun with what was left."

"You came up with all of these yourself?"

"Well no, not all of them. The blue one, here—well, it's the only blue one, so I suppose I didn't need to point to it. Anyway, the blue one was already a known substance. If put into the blood, it puts a person completely under, a bit like how the needles do, but deeper. It's useful when performing things like amputations. The person won't go to the bathroom for a few days though." He sniffed, then scratched the back of the head. "That's probably not worth noting."

"No, no, it's interesting." She crouched down and looked at the vials again. She pointed to the only blue one, then sarcastically asked, "Was this the blue one you were referring to?"

He didn't quite roll his eyes, but his slightly lifted brow looked like the tired man's equivalent.

Crossing his arms and leaning against a bookcase beside the desk, he welcomed more of her questions and answered them in detail. He explained that his fiend hunter alias was Yeltaire Veen, and that it'd allowed him to walk in and out of Sovereignty's main hospital without anyone realizing who he was.

"Nobody suspected it," he said. "Abaddon and I don't look much alike. I'm the brute, he's the prince. I'm fiendish, he's handsome. That sort of thing."

"I don't know if I'd say that."

Even avoiding his gaze, Rynara could tell Dietrich was smirking. She rose from where she'd been surveying the vials, and all the pieces of parchment strewn about the desk—barely legible scribbles Dietrich apparently considered notes—and turned away from him, not wanting the red of her face to match the vibrancy of the poisons.

"You'd say that if you saw him," he continued. "The little shit is quite beautiful."

"I have seen him," she replied, sitting down in one of the room's chairs. "Though I was quite a bit younger then. He was here in the West, with your father. I played the harp for him."

"Did he then learn how to play it just by watching you?"

She laughed. "No. He tried, though. He got very frustrated with the pedals."

"Sounds like him. I bet to this day he remembers that. He hates not being good at something. Hates it. I wouldn't be surprised if he begged our parents for a harp after that visit, just so he could try to get better than you."

Rynara took a breath, attempting to school her features. "You love him, after everything?"

Dietrich, still leaning against the bookshelf, turned slightly. He had one foot crossed over the other, and with his arms folded over his chest, he looked calm. It was only the slight working of his jaw and the tension in his neck that revealed his answer.

"Yes," he said softly. "I feel like I shouldn't, though. He killed our father. The idea of not *drifting* when you die? If you take your own life? It's a lie. If Abaddon ever bothered to take the critical eye he applies to everything else and use it, just once, on his own faith, he'd see that.

"When our people were enslaved, it was common for them to kill themselves. It wouldn't have mattered much to our captors, given that they themselves beat us to death frequently. What was one more dead serpent to them? It wasn't until the deaths were affecting their economy that they started to care."

Dietrich stopped suddenly, standing a little straighter. "I'm sorry. I'm telling you all of this, but you might already know."

Rynara shook her head. "I didn't know. Please." She held out her hand, beckoning him to continue.

He cleared his throat. "They placed Sadiyan priests and priestesses among the slaves. Not real priests, mind you. Or maybe at one time they *had* been real ones, but that's beside the point. The point is that the Prianthians had them spread the message among the other slaves that it was a slight against the Creator to take one's life—that if they did it, their souls wouldn't rest. It was the ultimate betrayal of the Creator's plan. It was a complete loss of faith."

"Light above," Rynara cursed, horrified. Then, realizing the irony, muttered, "Sorry."

Dietrich gave a one-shouldered shrug. "Bastard. Shit. Damn. It doesn't make a difference to me."

She gave him a weak smile, though she still felt guilty. Not just for the poorly chosen curse, but for everything awful in Sadie's past. The shackles that'd kept them chained, the heat that'd burned their skin, the boots that'd kept them down. The women who'd kept the population alive. The whips that'd lashed their backs.

Yet what words would be enough? There would never be enough apologies to make it right. She could never undo the past that'd befallen them. She couldn't rework the gears of time.

Sometimes she wished she could. Often, she wondered about her Amulet, about its ability to undo what'd been done, and she found herself musing on its untested powers. Could it only undo what'd been done in reference to the other Artifacts? Or could it reverse the effects of fate, of life itself, if she *called* upon it?

She wasn't meant to *call* on it, though. As a Guardian, she was meant to do the exact opposite: keep anyone from ever *calling* on it.

Absently, she reached up to her arm, rubbing at where the Amulet rested hidden beneath her clothes.

If she was forbidden to explore its powers, what was there to do when a descendant of atrocity stood before her? What broken parts of his nation now fell on him to repair? What parts of the soul had his father lost, all those years in chains, in rebellion, in leadership, that now had been passed on to him?

And my own father knew, she thought. *He'd known his actions were prolonging the Sadiyan's suffering, and he let it continue.*

"The Redeemers," she started. "They aren't entirely wrong. It doesn't justify what they're doing now, but I understand it."

Dietrich repositioned himself, stiffening. "What are you talking about?"

"That idea? Planting religious leaders among the populace? We did it here, in Xenith. We haven't done it in years, but the disparity between nobles and peasants used to be much wider. It should have led to a mass exodus of farmers and workmen, and without them, there'd be no one left to build the roads, or tend the farms, or whatever other things needed doing. The exodus never happened, though. For years, unless they were sent to war, people stayed. It's part of why Xenith and Mesidia are so homogenous.

"The Temple of the Stone, funded in part by lords, would preach to the peasants, tell them that if they were ever to leave their land or their homes, without the blessings of the Light—which only our priests could intercept, evidently—then when they died, their *auroras* would be lost, and rather than going to the Light, they'd *drift* endlessly, searching for the land they'd left behind."

"And Prianthia perfected the act," Dietrich concluded.

"Ironically," she said, shifting in her seat and lightening her voice. What she was about to say wasn't really ironic, but she found herself suddenly wanting to bring Dietrich back to his more carefree self. "I was, um—I was referring to this." She tapped her stomach. "The stabbing incident. When I asked if you still love Abaddon. But I appreciated the detour. I learned something valuable."

To her relief, he smiled. "Does this mean you believe me?"

"I believe it's very possible that if you've been on one of your never-ending chatter fests, someone might indeed try to stab you."

"A fine point. How my dear Seera hasn't set me ablaze yet, I'll never know."

"That poor creature. Her strength truly knows no bounds."

"Truly."

They stayed put for a moment, Dietrich still standing against the bookcase, practically in the very corner, Rynara seated, legs crossed, back straight. She knew she should tell him about Sovereignty, should pour alcohol on the wound and get it over with, but she still felt anxious. This man, if everything he said was to be believed, had endured so much already. It was bravery, in a sense, that he chose each day to quip and be merry and jest in defiance of the trials that sought to weigh him down.

She didn't want to contribute to those. Even if she was only the messenger.

"Would you like to sit?" She extended her foot and scooted the chair that sat opposite hers. "I'd feel less like a child about to be punished if you did."

"Is that a comment on our heights?"

"If by heights, you mean currently, with me sitting and you standing, then yes."

"I'm fine standing."

"I'd really prefer you sat."

"I don't like sitting."

Rynara rubbed her forehead.

"You don't like sitting?"

"I don't like sitting."

"Is this a new development? I recall you sitting very comfortably last night, when we were in the booth."

"That was different."

"How?"

"I picked a booth in the corner. And there was alcohol."

Rynara half sighed, half growled. "Do you have any alcohol on your person? Or somewhere in this room?"

"I do not."

"So you'll stand, for eternity, until you die?"

"Certainly not. I will sleep at some point. I just . . . have an aversion to chairs."

"I see that."

He lifted his hands. "People have snuck up on me more times than I can count. I've also been tied up in a chair. And not in the exciting way."

"What's the exciting way?"

Dietrich gave her a pointed look.

"Oh."

"Is that not as common in the West? Or among nobles? It's not entirely uncommon in Sadie, surprisingly. There's a whole market for it, especially in the brothels. Sometimes people like to act out certain roles, one person being the powerful one, the other submissive. It's very popular among the older generations, believe it or not. They feel like they're mocking the Prianthians, claiming power over what they once feared—I'm very surprised you're not frantically waving for me to stop."

Rynara swallowed. "I suppose it's important for me to . . . become more enlightened, regarding other cultures and peoples."

"If you really want to be enlightened, I am happy to provide a demonstration."

"Just sit in the chair, please."

Smug, and with a face much less red than her own, Dietrich walked over, pushed the chair up against the shelves he'd been leaning on and, finally, took a seat.

Taking a breath, Rynara retrieved the day's printing from the pocket of her vest and slowly unfolded it.

She read over the article again, willing the words to change, wishing she'd simply misread them, that Dietrich's home hadn't welcomed in the very enemies he'd dedicated most of his life to keeping at bay.

"I got this at the meeting," she said. "A man named Gregor gave it to me. Abaddon still hasn't woken up. The group of Prianthian soldiers who've been waiting outside the capital have been allowed into Sovereignty."

She watched him for a moment. It seemed intrusive, studying him, waiting for his reaction, so she looked back at the printing, smoothed out the creases, then set it on the small tea table between them.

Dietrich licked his lips. After a moment, he leaned forward and took the printing, read it over, folded it back up, and tossed it back onto the table.

"I'm sorry." It was all she could think to say. She folded her hands in her lap.

"Why? Did you let them in?"

It was said with levity, but Rynara could hear the bite in the words. Not at her—she had to remind herself. It was so obviously not at her that the reminder felt needless, but after years of her father's anger being improperly placed, it seemed important she make efforts to not put onto others what her father had put onto her.

"No," she answered softly. "I'm sorry all the same. Will you be going back?"

Dietrich shook his head, a sad smile cutting his face. "I can't. I've been exiled."

"That doesn't matter."

"Do you want me to go back?"

"No, I . . ." She stopped, realizing she'd scooted to the edge of her seat, furious on Dietrich's behalf. She couldn't imagine what it must be like to have her own family know of her innocence and still deem her exiled. "If you want to go back, then you should. Sadie is your home. You shouldn't let a label, a falsely given one, keep you from returning.

"But if you don't want to go back, then don't. You can stay here and help us fight the Redeemers. If we don't stop them here, I imagine their influence in the West is only going to build. We could use your help."

She leaned forward, elbows resting on her knees. "You also don't have to help anyone. You can live for yourself now, if that's what you'd like. You've already done so much for Sadie, and for the brief time you were here before, you did much for Voradeen. I don't think any of it would be standing if not for your efforts."

She stopped, letting her words settle. Realization dawned on her, how similar her statements were to the conversation with Luthier. The difference, of course, was how much Dietrich had done. Sure, she might've fought alongside him during the Attack of Fiends, but that was her own city, and that was the only real act of importance she'd taken on behalf of her country. Before that, she studied Abra'am's history, trained with her knights, mastered her harp, then her elements, then her swordsmanship. She'd admired old paintings that'd lined the palace and castle halls. She'd read books in her library. Consumed delicious food. Drank expensive wine.

How did that compare to what Dietrich had done? He'd lived most of his adolescence on the streets of his city, separated from his family and the comforts of their palace. He'd had no coin, no one to prepare food for him, no one to keep him safe. He'd killed his first man when he was barely more than a boy, then he'd been expected to continue killing when he'd barely been more than a man.

He'd done all of that while still finding time to help his brother create cures, master poison work, study fiends, and set out on whatever fanciful quests his family sent him on.

"You could do the same," he said, after a long stretch of silence. "What keeps you from stopping?"

"My brother," she said instinctively. "I think I'd be much more tempted to stop, if he wasn't still in the palace. A part of me wants to protect him. Another part of me, selfishly, wants him to know I didn't do it. I didn't kill our father. He might . . . hear things about how my father treated me when I was younger. Some of the servants might tell him about what they overheard, the bruises they saw. It stopped, mostly, after a couple years, before Aden could've really retained anything, but given how little he saw my father and me interacting, he wouldn't have much to counter the statements, if they did make their way to him."

Dietrich's hands formed fists. "Your father abused you?"

"He didn't abuse me," she said defensively. "He would get angry sometimes, and when I went to him, he'd sometimes, I don't know, he'd push me aside, but harder than he meant to. I think he forgot how small I was."

"Did he hit you?"

She glared at him.

"He only struck my face once. He'd never hit me like that before, though. But it's irrelevant, because I was—"

"Irrelevant?" Dietrich interrupted. "I believe you came here to inform me of the meeting you had, and yet we spent a great deal of time discussing, let's see. . . ." He held up his hand, tapping his fingers. "Poisons, to start. Religion as a weapon of control. Chairs. A good roll around with ropes—"

"I wouldn't say we spent a great deal of time on that."

"Not to mention when we were supposed to be discussing the Sanctuary last night, we talked about meedla and sandmilk, waking up at Light-forsaken hours, and the merits of describing me as a stalker."

He lowered his hand, eyes softening.

"We stray from topics, but not quite as intentionally as you're doing now. And that's fine. If you don't want to talk about this, we don't have to. If you don't want to call what happened to you abuse, then we don't have to call it that. We can talk about something else."

He twirled his finger in the air, as though he were pulling an idea to his mind.

"How was the meeting?" he offered. "Are you all right after what happened at the clock tower today? Can we both agree that the fourth chime was too early?"

He attempted a smile.

"If there's ever anything you don't want to go into detail about, then don't. Just tell me you don't want to, and I'll leave it be. But you don't need to try and diminish what's been done to you. I don't know if you were doing it for yourself or for my sake—but please, *especially* don't do it for my sake. Just . . . Just know it's all right to be angry. I haven't known you very long, but you seem like you're constantly angry anyway, just usually on behalf of the wrongs done to others. You're allowed to let others be angry on behalf of the wrongs done to you."

Her face grew hot. "But I just told you what happened to your home. I should be comforting you."

She heard her voice crack, and her fingers started to tremble. Frustrated, she folded her lips in, inhaled deeply through her nose, and squeezed her eyes shut.

Desperation pressed just beneath the surface of her skin, a desperation to let everything out, to let everything come freely through her eyes, her nose, her throat. It was almost painful now, keeping it all back.

It was childish, she thought, that she wanted to cry at all.

Dietrich, seeming to realize she hadn't finished her point and that she was making an effort to collect herself, kept quiet.

"He did it a long time ago," she finally said. "The pain is old. It's not pressing, and it only impacts me. Everything going on with the Redeemers? That affects thousands of people. It affects you. That's what we should be focusing on. That's what *I* should be focusing on."

"Are we doing anything tonight?"

She sniffed. "What?"

"Tonight," he repeated. "Your little army. Are we going through with any plans tonight?"

"No."

"You don't have to feel guilty then, talking about something that affects you. There's nothing else we have to be doing right now."

He *called* a flame element, igniting the fireplace in the space between and beside their chairs. The sun had mostly gone down, and while twilight still kept some light in the sky, Rynara hadn't realized just how dark the room had become until the fire started.

"Unless you'd rather not," he added, settling back in his seat. "There's plenty more to discuss. But trust me, if you think it's a great burden for me to do the listening rather than the talking, I assure you, it's not."

She gave an uneven wobble of her head, pretending to mull the point over.

"All right."

She licked her lips, unsure where to start.

"I don't know why I can't stop thinking about it. When it was happening, I could forget about it immediately after. He was away a lot, and when he left, I was relieved. Then, when he came back, I'd find myself happy again. I loved him and I missed him, and each time he returned, I hoped he'd come back the way he'd been before my mother had died. He'd been happier, then. I just wanted him be happy again. Everything had been good before. I figured everything has to be good again eventually, right?

"And things were getting better. He was controlling his anger more. And now..."

She choked on the words, her face heating, her fingers digging into her leggings.

"And now he's gone. I finally had him back, if only for a bit, and now he's dead, and I'm angry at him for being dead, even though I know that doesn't make any sense. I'm mad, but I'm a bit relieved too, and I hate myself for feeling like that because I loved him. He was my father. He was just a person, and I know he loved me."

She stopped, catching her breath, realizing she'd started quickening her words to the point that she'd stopped breathing.

"I suppose I just keep hoping I can go back. That feeling I'd have, when he'd leave, and I hoped he'd come back a little bit better? Something in my mind keeps thinking that's my reality. I keep forgetting that someday, when I do finally go back to Voradeen, he won't be there.

"But that's all I want. I want to be home, waiting for my father to come back, and for him to remember that I miss my mother too. I don't know how to help raise Aden without her around. I need help. I need him to help me.

"I feel like my life started over when he died, and I don't know how to live without him. Sometimes I don't even know if I want to."

A tear fell from her eye. She couldn't have stopped it, eager as it was to be free.

She wiped at the streak it left, irritated. It was one thing to reveal her thoughts. It was another thing entirely to reveal how those thoughts crippled her, sank her, pulled her into the depths. She swallowed again. Sniffed. Pulled her sleeve down past her wrist and dabbed at her nose.

She did whatever she could not to look at Dietrich.

Hearing him stand, she let her eyes drift to his feet, watching as they crossed the room.

They stopped in front of her.

She finally looked up.

"There's no poison on it, if that's what you're wondering." He held out a kerchief. She took it with a mumbled thanks, dabbing it to her nose, then, more discreetly, at the streaks tears had left.

Dietrich walked over to the fire. He crouched down to it, his back turned to her. He had something in his hands. She hadn't noticed him grab it, whatever it was, while she'd tended to her cheeks and nose and eyes, but when he turned around, she saw it was a blanket, one that'd been draped across the back of his desk chair.

Wordlessly, he walked back over to her and wrapped the blanket around her shoulders.

She imagined she made a rather sore sight, huddled into herself, enveloped by the warmed blanket. She likely resembled an elderly woman who found a light breeze comparable to an arctic blast.

It was when Dietrich pulled both ends of the blanket around her front, and kneeled before her, green eyes filled with some emotion she couldn't name, that she finally let her tears fall freely.

He leaned forward, letting her head fall against his shoulder, arms wrapping around her. Tall as he was, with her seated in a chair, and his knees planted firmly on the floor, he was still nearly even with her. The realization oddly amused her, even through the sadness that was spilling out.

He didn't shush her. He didn't whisper empty platitudes. There were no reassurances that everything would be fine. He couldn't promise her that, and it wouldn't have made her feel better anyway. They'd both seen too much in their lives to know such words weren't true.

"Do you want some tea?" he asked, when her sobs had quieted. "Or a hot bath? I can bring in a washbasin, if you'd like to wash your face."

"Tea would be nice," she said weakly. "But . . . is there a tea you like? Something Sadiyan?"

Dietrich pulled away, giving her wrists a reassuring squeeze. He didn't ask her why she wanted something Sadiyan. He only answered, "Sure," with a quick smile before getting up to make it.

The quiet after a cry, especially after one in front of a person you weren't all that close to, was strange. All the little noises in the room stood out, as though they were being amplified by the pure silence of the two humans present. The fire was certainly not roaring, but the small crackles seemed as though they were hints of an explosion about to happen. The sounds of the tea being made were a small chamber orchestra, made up solely of unskilled musicians who couldn't quite keep rhythm.

The city lamps were alighting outside the window, as were the people of Sarabai who were already enjoying the end of their workday with wine-induced reverie.

Rynara almost wished she'd taken Dietrich up on his chair demonstration offer, thinking sex might've been less intimate than whatever she'd just let happen. She wrapped the blanket around herself tighter, as though that could block out her embarrassment, but when Dietrich returned with the tea, warm voice stating, "It's quite hot," she found it wasn't as difficult to meet his eye as she'd expected.

He grabbed his chair with one hand and lifted it back over to its original spot. He sat down, blowing on his tea. He took a sip, eyes toward the fire.

"Thank you," Rynara said, clearing her throat. "The tea is very good."

"Our head watchman, Culter, used to make it for Abaddon and me. I miss him. I saw him when I"—he looked into his cup—"I saw him recently. It made me homesick. I hadn't felt like that, being at the palace, or seeing my brother, or walking through Sovereignty again. All of that had felt like a mirage. Seeing Culter again, though, made it all real. I think for the first time, I really understood what I was doing in letting everyone believe I'd tried to kill my own brother. It'd never really sunk in until I saw the horror in Culter's eyes."

He took another drink of tea, wincing at how hot it was, then wiped his mouth.

"Anyway, he liked this tea. It could taste like shit, for all I know, but it makes me think of him, so I can't tell the difference."

"It's good," Rynara reassured. "Really."

They sat in silence again for a time, both drinking their tea. It was a companionable silence. She couldn't remember the last time she'd had that.

"I hope this doesn't come out wrong," Dietrich started, "but so much of what you said, I've felt before too. All of it. I remember a moment of time, when I was young, before the Redeemers came, when all I really knew was my father and mother happy, and Abaddon being good at everything, and Sovereignty being"—he snapped his fingers, trying to find a suitable word—"alive, I suppose. Everyone was happy. People were kind and generous. People were always shouting too, but not in anger. It was like every day was a celebration. I suppose it was, for a lot of them.

"And then the Redeemers came. It was like a plague. Nobody died, obviously, not that first night, but it was like everything darkened.

"My life started over when I made my first kill. I kept feeling like, I don't know . . . like if I could just kill them all, then I could go back to that old Sadie.

"I think my brother felt it too. I think he figured if he could heal everyone, and make us so valuable as a nation that we'd have allies everywhere, then we could all go back.

"We never spoke of it, but I saw it in the way he was always working, always looking for a new cure, always losing sleep."

Rynara slid from the chair to the rug beneath it, scooting closer to the fire.

"I don't think there's anything wrong with what you said," she told him. "I can't imagine what that was like."

"I didn't want you to think I was trying to topple your admission," he said, drinking the rest of his tea in one large gulp. "I've met people like that. The moment you reveal something of yourself, all they want to do is wait until you're done so they can talk about themselves. I didn't want you to think that's what I was doing."

She smiled, and said quietly, "I didn't think that."

"Good. Good. I was only wanting to say that I . . . that what you said, I've never heard someone say that in a way that was so similar to what I knew. How I felt. How I *still* feel. And I suppose, I figured, if it made me feel a little less alone, maybe it would make you feel a little less alone too, knowing a bit about . . . a bit about me."

He returned her smile, then placed his now empty cup on the table, removed his gloves, angled his chair toward the fire, and warmed his hands.

"I used to be jealous of you," Rynara confessed. "When I was younger. I used to think your life sounded amazing. You were a prince, and you got to roam about your city, taking out an evil uprising, with no one knowing it was you? It was like a real-life version of the heroes I read about in books. I think I actually wanted to *be* you. I think maybe that's what I'm doing now."

"How's that going for you?"

She leaned back, squinting and *hmm*-ing loudly. She uncurled her legs, stretching.

"Oh, you know, it's completely divine. Everyone loves me. I can come and go where and when I please. I'll admit that the horrible acts of violence can be a bit alarming, but you take the good with the bad."

He kicked her booted foot. "I know you're jesting, but it does have its perks."

"What was the worst part for you? You said the other day ... wait, no, last night. Has it really only been a night? Anyway, you said you slept in hay barns and stables. I'd imagine, in the summer especially, that was rather difficult."

"It wasn't so bad. The stables especially. I always enjoyed being around horses. They never got spooked by me, surprisingly. And the stable boys—or girls, occasionally—would play cards with me, or dice. It reminded me of when Abaddon and I were boys.

"I think the worst part was never having anyone know who I was. Always feeling like, no matter how close I was to someone, they'd never really know me. Not entirely. It made me feel like I was always living a lie, even when everything else I said, or every other part of how I was around another person, was the truth. There was something about when they'd say my name, whatever false name I'd given them, that I'd be reminded I was alone."

Rynara nodded. She'd only been living as this version of herself for a short time, and already she understood. At least she had Luthier, who might call her Rynara, but who knew that was only a false name. He kept her anchored, in some small way, to who she really was, what she stood for, what she was trying to do. Dietrich had still occasionally seen his family, but for most of his life, from one day to the next, one week to the next, he had only himself. That part, that level of solitude, she wasn't sure she could ever truly comprehend.

Setting her cup down beside his, she gently tapped her booted foot against his leg.

"When we're alone, you can call me Gwenivere, and I'll call you Dietrich. We'll remind each other. Unless you'd prefer not to of course."

He stared at her a moment, fingers clenching and unclenching. She saw his chest rise and fall once, twice, three times, his eyes nearly aglow from the brightness of the fire.

"That's a fine idea, Lady Gwenivere," he said.

When the sun had completely set, and twilight had given way to night, Rynara informed Dietrich of everything discussed during the meeting. They agreed he'd eventually have to reveal himself to the others. He'd go by Yeltaire Veen, when he did. He was used to that name. He'd respond to it.

Though the plan hadn't come together yet, he decided he'd get to work on studying substances that might cause smoke, or an irritating gas—anything that might be able to be set off inside the Sanctuary, to make everyone evacuate. He was rather certain he could come up with something if he started working on it now. Rynara asked to be given some of the books he'd apparently gotten recently from Sarabai's library, realizing now that many of the books in the bookcase he'd been huddling himself against were not decor but texts he'd been studying.

Despite how little he'd slept the night before, Dietrich's nocturnal instincts seemed to kick in, and his energy came to him the longer the night went on. Rynara, however, never having been one for the darker hours, nor really being able to make heads or tails of what they were studying, found her eyelids were heavy, then drooping, then closed.

She remembered being picked up at some point and protesting slightly, then ending her protest when, after a moment, she was planted gently into a very soft, very warm bed. She awoke a few times, dark images forcing her from her sleep. Sometimes they were of a head removed from its body. Sometimes they were her father's *auroras*, so far away but still visibly *ascending*. Other times, it was her city, her capital, burned to the ground by the Behemoth.

Each time, she need only to gain her bearings, see Dietrich in the room's corner, on the floor, with several books open around him, to return to sleep.

In the morning, when the sun began rising over the city's buildings, Rynara woke up, and stayed awake. She found Dietrich fast asleep on the floor, his long body curled tight, now that the fire had died. She remembered mumbling something about the Attack of Fiends to him, after one of her nightmares during the night. She remembered him exchanging the fire for a lamp. She felt guilty for that now, seeing him asleep on the floor, clearly cold and likely uncomfortable.

She rose from the bed and grabbed the blanket he'd given her, and another from the bed, and placed them both over him. She brought a pillow over too, but settled on putting it beside him, afraid she'd wake him if she tried getting his head under it. At least it was there, she told herself, if he rustled a bit and sleepily managed to get it where he wanted. He'd likely be awake enough to move to the bed if that happened, but the option was there, if he needed it.

Making as little noise as she could, she grabbed her boots and cloak—two things she'd taken off during her attempt at helping him study—then she gently turned the door's handle and walked out of the room.

CHAPTER FIFTY-FOUR
RYNARA

Without gaining entry into the Sanctuary, the Hawks were at a standstill.

Each new meeting, they argued how best to take it over. All the members of Rynara's circle—which included Dietrich, though she still hadn't introduced him to the others—had observed the Sanctuary, yet none of them could agree on how to liberate it.

Rynara and Dietrich had only seen three guards at the entrance, but since their visit and the death of the tradesmen, those numbers had gone up.

The upside was that the Redeemers within Sarabai itself seemed to have lessened. Fewer kidnappings had occurred, trade of illegal substances hadn't been spotted in over a week, and according to the enforcers working for Rynara, no murders had been reported.

The city had been saved.

Now Rynara needed to save those who'd been taken from it.

The most lawful position was informing the enforcers of

the Sanctuary's locations. None of the Hawks favored this idea, given how corrupt the enforcers were. If they were notified of the Sanctuary's location, it might just result in her showing her hand and losing any leverage she'd gained.

Rynara's preferred plan was training the new recruits for a unified attack. More had joined the Hawks in recent weeks. If they gained enough members, she could lead them against the Sanctuary herself, rather than hoping the enforcers would do it.

That idea came with flaws, of course. The biggest was in thinking that the number of guards stationed outside the Sanctuary—twenty had been the largest amount seen by the Hawks—was their entire retinue. It was likely more guards resided inside, and, given how long they'd had their hideout in the caves, they might know additional exits to escape from.

The issue of kidnappees also came up. With a fight coming straight on, the Redeemers might threaten the lives of those they'd taken, regardless of the fact that said kidnappees were their workforce. There was no way to know if the Redeemers might send their slaves out to face off against the Hawks, rather than coming out themselves.

Though it wasn't entirely a problem, Teniv had also pointed out the amount of time it would take to carry out the plan. Luthier didn't feel confident that the new recruits would be ready for at least a few months, and the longer they waited, the more time people were kept in the Redeemers' hands.

Knowing all that, Rynara still favored that plan over the one the Hawks currently decided was best.

Sending Luthier in.

It was a simple plan: Allow Luthier to be caught, then send him notes through the cracks in the cave's ceiling. Already Rynara and the Hawks had been back to the Sanctuary, surveying it from the land above, and they agreed that someone skilled enough with *calling* air could try and spot Luthier and send notes down to him. So long as he was 'captured' with a bit of charcoal on his person, or if they sent charcoal down alongside the notes, he'd be able to write about what he discovered and gain them the valuable information they needed, such as who all was in the Sanctuary, how many trained guards were there, if the slaves had fighting experience.

So on and so on.

It was a good plan, and Luthier was willing to do it.

Rynara just wasn't willing to let him.

Not yet, at least.

We'll train the new recruits for another month, she'd said. *We'll see how well their progressing. If they don't seem ready by then, we'll consider sending Luthier in.*

She'd explained the situation to Dietrich. Even without opening up to him about how much she hadn't wanted to let Luthier go, he'd seemed to figure it out.

Garron is your Culter, he'd said. *The watchman I mentioned to you? The one who trained me? He was like a second father to me. He was a father to me, in a lot of ways. Your knight is that for you, I suspect?*

You suspect correctly.

Let's try to find another way, then, shall we?

When she wasn't hosting meetings, or watching the training with the new recruits, or managing any one of the many things she did as the Phoenix, Rynara spent her time in Dietrich's rooms, trying to come up with another course of action.

She was surprised at how tirelessly he worked. While the Redeemers had been his main enemies for most of his adult life, the goings on in Sarabai didn't feel like his battle. Saving Luthier certainly didn't feel like his battle, yet there he was, every night, every day, and, to her surprise, even on most mornings, hunched over his notes and his books and his poisons, trying to find her another path.

Despite knowing next to nothing about his work, Rynara poured herself into it. If he was searching for the properties of a certain herb, she'd reference every book on his shelf or head to Sarabai's several libraries to try and find what she could on it.

If she found something, but couldn't determine whether it was useful, she'd mark the page, then stack the book onto his desk for him to flip through later.

Sometimes her tasks were a little less academic. She'd hold vials for him as he mixed different liquids together, or she'd write things down as he conducted experiments.

Other times, she simply brought him something to eat.

"I'm trying to figure out a way to replicate what my needles do," he explained to her, bending over so he was eye level with one of his vials. "Specifically, if I can replicate the effect through the air, and for only a short period of time, I think we might have something. We could distribute the gas through the cracks, and while everyone is out, your Hawks could get in, retrieve the slaves, and get out. Once everyone is safe, we could destroy it, or turn it over to the enforcers—whatever you want to do. As long as we get the innocents out, it doesn't really matter what happens to the building or the people left in it."

"Do you think you're close to making that happen?"

Dietrich cursed as the liquid dripped onto his finger, burning his skin.

"If I have a month, I think I can make something."

It had been nearly a month. They only had a few days left, and the new recruits definitely weren't ready.

If Dietrich couldn't figure something out, Luthier was going in.

Rynara rubbed her eyes. She was reading through a text on dangerous gases. Apparently, people couldn't go through certain swamps without dousing and wrapping kerchiefs around their faces like masks, though the finer details confused her.

She was tired, and the lamps they'd been using grew dim. Current metal often needed to be recharged, which would happen at the inn at the end of the week, but until then, the lamps the metal were powering in their rooms would continue to dim.

Normally it wasn't much of an issue, as residents didn't usually light lamps for the entire night, but with how much Dietrich had been working and the hours he often chose to work, they'd run through them quicker than was typical.

The fireplace had been blazing at the start of the night. Now there was nothing left but a few embers.

Deciding it best to rest her eyes and get Dietrich's opinion, Rynara yawned and scratched her neck. When she blinked a few times and looked around the room, she saw Dietrich was on the floor a few feet away, sitting against a bookshelf with his knees tucked close to his chest. He had a book propped up to read, but his eyes were closed, and his head rested again the wall.

Rynara didn't want to wake him. She'd barely gone to her own rooms the last few weeks, never wanting to stop assisting his work, so she knew firsthand how little he'd slept. Always, with how accustomed she was to morning hours, she fell asleep before him, and, through some miraculous force of will and a great deal of sundrops, she'd even discovered Dietrich had been waking up before her.

Granted, he was practically falling over at the end of his work and would fall asleep quickly after. He also didn't have anywhere he needed to be during the day, but still. He'd woken her up a few too many mornings by bumping into something after his eyes had completely lost focus.

You really can't be doing that with all those poisons in here! she'd scolded one morning.

He'd mumbled an apology, but hadn't done anything in the way of getting more rest.

Looking at him now, Rynara wondered how often he'd fallen asleep in such a position. He'd told her multiple stories about the strange places he'd slept in. Rooftops were his favorites, as he liked being up high, where he could look at both his city beneath him, and the stars above, but sometimes he found himself crammed between wine barrels, or beneath carts—anywhere tight and hidden—where pursuers weren't likely to spot him.

Sleep didn't appear peaceful for him. He didn't toss and turn as Rynara did, nor did he make much noise, but there was an apprehension to him, like he was an animal about to be slaughtered. Rynara remembered watching deer when she'd hunted with Garron in the forests outside her castle. If she made a noise, the deer would perk up, still and tense, body ready to spring into flight.

That's how Dietrich looked to her. Was it because he truly never felt safe when his body was succumbing to the vulnerability of sleep, or was it because of what lay in his dreams?

She almost thought he woke for a moment as the tendon in his neck flexed and his folded arms tightened. She startled, quietly taking a quick breath, but he wasn't awake.

He was having a nightmare.

Careful not to frighten him, Rynara grabbed the blanket she'd draped over her lap, rested her book on the tea table, and carefully lowered herself to the floor. Making sure not to let her chair legs screech, she came to the floor slowly, then nudged forward. When she'd crossed over to him, she lifted the blanket, and gently made to rest it over his legs.

His eyes opened.

Her hand was smacked aside.

Her body was thrown against the floor, knocking the air out of her.

A knife was pulled from a sheath—from where, she didn't know. It happened so quick, her sleep-addled mind barely registered what was happening before he was on top of her, and the hand holding the knife hurled toward her neck.

"Dietrich!"

He halted. The knife rested inches from her skin.

She could hardly breathe. His free arm pressed against her throat. His chest heaved.

"Dietrich," she soothed. "It's me. Gwenivere."

His eyes, bloodshot and wide, seemed to finally see her. The *touched* knife clattered to floor. He pulled back from her, his face contorted.

"I'm sorry," he whispered. He sat on his knees. His breaths were ragged. "Gwen, I'm so sorry."

"It's all right," she assured, feeling terrible. "Dietrich, calm down. It's all right."

"I almost killed you."

"I wouldn't have let you."

"You don't know that."

"Dietrich." She inched closer, looking him dead in the eye. "I'm fine."

He stood, seeming almost . . . ashamed. He grabbed the *touched* knife from the floor and returned it to its sheath, then began the process of removing all the *touched* knives from his person.

Rynara sat quietly, her back facing the fire. Even with how little remained, it still emitted a pleasant heat.

"I'm sorry," she said softly. "I was only trying to help."

Dietrich had been letting each knife drop to his desk with a loud, furious thump, but at that, he removed the last one, and set it down softly.

"You have nothing to be sorry for."

He finally turned to face her, making his way back to the floor and sitting beside her. She hadn't realized it, but she'd pulled her legs up to her chest and wrapped her arms around them, trying to take up less space.

Cautiously, Dietrich reached out to her. She looked at him, confused, then let him take her hand.

"You did nothing wrong," he said. "I was ashamed of myself, but I didn't realize how my anger might remind you of your youth."

Rynara almost pulled her hand back. She made an effort to cool her nerves and force away her defensive impulse.

She closed her eyes. He was still holding her hand. His thumb brushed across her skin, letting her know he was there, and he wasn't upset.

Not at her.

"You were having a nightmare," she said, opening her eyes. "I thought you were anyway. I tried to give you this."

She felt stupid as she took her hand back and picked up the blanket, plopping it on the rug between them.

Dietrich wrapped the blanket around her shoulders.

She stopped him.

"No," she said. "You need to sleep."

"I will. I just need to—"

"No." She rose, let the blanket fall, and reached out her hand. "Come on. You're exhausted. We'll start again in the morning."

He chuckled, then took her hand.

"Am I a child being put to bed?"

"Yes."

When he rose, she found herself taken aback by his height. He still had his shoes on, and she'd taken hers off hours ago, but regardless, his full height always seemed to surprise her.

"You're going to sleep too I presume?" he asked.

She swallowed. "I might retire soon. I still have some energy."

"If I'm being forced to sleep, you have to sleep too."

He smiled.

She frowned.

She didn't know why she felt so warm, suddenly. She stepped back, holding her hand out to his bed as if presenting it.

"I'll retire soon," she repeated.

He nodded, then, rather than making his way to his bed, began unfastening his vest.

Her eyes widened before she quickly looked away. After his vest would come his shirt, likely. That was how he opened the door that one morning, after all—without a shirt.

Light, was this really the first time he'd gone to sleep before her? By the time she woke up, he was either still awake, or had already risen, and he wouldn't head to sleep again until after she left. It was completely normal for a person to be in some state of undress before sleep, but she hadn't thought about that until now, given that she'd always fallen asleep accidentally, when she was fully dressed and sitting on the rug beside the fire, or curled up in a chair, or laying on her stomach atop the bed, a book propped up on a pillow.

"Gwenivere?"

"Yes?"

"Have you fallen asleep standing?"

She opened her eyes, not realizing she'd squeezed them shut.

"Um, no, sorry. I was just trying to give you privacy."

Her eyes flicked to his general direction for a moment, long enough to note he still had his trousers on, but that his shirt and vest and shoes had been removed.

"We've addressed this before, I believe," he said, walking past her. She kept her eyes forward.

"Addressed what?"

"That I have nothing here worth noting."

"I don't recall addressing that."

"When you woke me up at that Light-forsaken hour? When we first went to the Sanctuary?"

"Ah, yes, right."

She finally mustered up the courage to look at him, annoyed to find all his previous guilt and shame gone as he leaned against the bedframe, arms across his chest.

She locked her jaw, determined not to look at the dark scars on his stomach, or any of the other scars, or any other part of him besides his face.

"Sleep," she ordered. "Go to sleep."

She pointed to the bed as though he was a dog who'd be rewarded as soon as he went where he was meant to go.

He glanced down, cheeks dimpled slightly, but the expression faded when he looked back up and met her gaze.

"I'm sorry," he said. "Really. I don't know that I can go to sleep without knowing that you're all right."

Lowering her pointing finger, she let her hands fall to her sides, and curled her toes.

"It was a bit disconcerting, when you walked away. I don't know how you could sense that, though. I think I'm embarrassed, more than anything. I feel like I've ruined the night."

"You didn't."

"I feel like it," she insisted. She scrunched her mouth, one eye squinting as she clucked her tongue. "It's quite ridiculous. I know it is. I didn't care at all that you . . ."

She'd been about to say *attacked me*, then thought better of it.

"That you'd pinned me down," she said. "That's the part that should've frightened me. I know that. I suppose I'm just confused at what my body deems a threat and what it doesn't."

She expected Dietrich to crack a smile and make a jest, but instead he stared at her intently. His eyes made her uneasy, though in a completely different way than they had before. It was something in the way they held hers, not with anger, or with question, but in acknowledgment.

Unfolding his arms, he held a hand out to her. She stared at it, then at him, unsure of the gesture but choosing to trust him.

As she took it, he pulled her toward him and enveloped her in an embrace.

She tensed. She was rarely ever held like this. She was rarely ever held at all. Embraces from her father, for many years, had come after hurt and were accompanied with justifications. *You know I only want what's best for you. You know I just want you safe.*

Luthier rarely held her at all. It seemed a miracle he'd been as open as he was after the meeting at the warehouse. That alone had felt like an embrace, for how little her knight normally shared his thoughts and emotions. To pour out such a soft memory had been the warmest hug she could imagine from him.

This, though—this tight, encircling hold, not when she was crying, but when she was merely herself—was different. It seemed a friendly thing, and an intimate thing, and a thing of innocence all wrapped in one.

When she let her arms fold around him, it seemed a freeing

thing too. For all she'd shared with him and all that'd been discussed between them, there was something all-together different about sharing touch.

She thought to pull away, but she'd been a woman starved, just given food. She wasn't ready to let go so quickly. She stepped closer, squeezing him tighter, her shoulders sagging with some unknown relief when he rested his head atop hers.

"I thought you'd make a stupid comment," she said.

"Me? Never. I'm only ever dignified."

"Need I remind you that you called the caves 'The Serpent's Farts?'"

He chuckled. The low sound rumbled through his chest, and Rynara smiled, enjoying the experience of holding someone as they laughed.

"Young Dietrich called them that. You cannot hold me to the things he said."

She pulled away, smiling as she met his gaze. He was smiling too, and she expected him to say more or thought she herself would say more, but when he was silent, she found she didn't have the will to speak.

He still held her. Her arms were no longer encircling him, but her hands rested against the sides of his stomach.

She cleared her throat and stepped back.

"Sleep, then," she said. "You may rest well. I am at ease now, I promise."

His hands rested against the bed's frame. She tried not to immediately look away, though it felt unusual, to purposefully let herself view his naked torso as a means of pretending she *wasn't* noticing his naked torso.

"What were you reading?" he asked. "That you feel so compelled to continue on?"

She opened her mouth to answer, then glowered when she couldn't remember.

"I honestly don't recall."

He smiled, then took his turn to gesture to the bed in the same awkward way she had before.

"Sleep, then?"

"I told *you* to sleep."

"I intend to."

"Yes, but *you* should sleep in your bed."

"I intend to."

"Yes, but you're—oh."

Oh. Yes, that made sense. She'd slept in that bed most nights, and it was certainly big enough for them both. Her own bed hadn't warmed her in weeks, and it would seem like she was making a fuss over nothing if his presence a foot away from her sent her stomping over to it.

She didn't want him to think her flustered over their hug.

Or his partially undressed form.

He'd certainly think that if she left.

Batting his hand away, she walked to the side of the bed she usually claimed, and began undoing the buttons of her own vest. He climbed into the bed, and she expected him to pull the blankets over his head and turn away with a cheerful *Good night*, but the thought seemed more a wish than an actual expectation.

What he *actually* did was rest one hand on his stomach, and the other behind his head.

Suddenly, she didn't feel as tired.

"Swamps," she said. "I'd been reading about swamps."

He peeled open a single eye, the corner of his mouth lifting. "And?"

She undressed hurriedly, pulling off the cuffs around her arms, and the belt from her hip. She grabbed the shirt Dietrich had tossed to the floor and put it on—over hers, which didn't make much sense—then shimmied out of her trousers, grateful now that he was so damnably tall, and that his shirt came down practically to her knees.

"Some swamps are poisonous," she said, swiftly ducking beneath the sheets once she'd pulled her shirt out from under the long one. "There are things in the air that are dangerous if breathed in. I marked the page. We can go over it in the morning."

His shirt smelled like him, a scent she'd just gotten a lot of, given their hug. It was something Sadiyan—his own washing soaps, rather than the inn's—a combination of sandalwood and some pleasant spice, mixed with the wood of the fire, the pages of the book, and a bit of the potions he was always working on.

The scent was soothing, she realized, which made her pull the blankets up higher, and clutch them tighter.

"Ahem. Gwen?"

"Yes."

"Do I get any of those?"

She bolted upright, seeing that she'd pulled all the blankets to her side. He was completely without cover, and still lay in that same position. Both eyes were open now, and his grin looked far more amused than it had any reason to be.

"Sorry," she mumbled. She'd been about to hand some covers over, then decided she was done letting him always do the unraveling. She wanted him to be uneasy, for a change. She wanted to be the mischievous one, smirking at his discomfort.

Hoisting the blankets even further to her side, she turned away, snuggled comfortably with her pillow, and muttered, "Is that better?"

"So no, then? I don't get any?"

"Sorry, no. I'm very small and have very low body heat. I'm much like Seera: I don't do well with the cold."

She made an obnoxiously loud sound of contentment.

Truthfully, she loved the cold, but this was worth it. With how easy it was for him to constantly make fun of her and cause her cheeks to redden, she was finally getting her revenge.

It failed when his arm wrapped around her stomach, and his chest pressed against her back.

"Like Seera?" he asked. There was an intense heat, and she realized that he'd *called* warmth to his hand. She stopped breathing when his fingers found her skin between the buttons of the shirt.

"Yup," she forced out with feigned nonchalance. It took her a moment to puzzle out what he was doing, and she inwardly cursed herself when she put it together.

The dragon enjoyed her scales warmed and rubbed through with his *auroras*.

He rested his head against her pillow.

Her pillow. Not his.

She supposed that's what she got for stealing the covers.

"Are you still wearing your stockings?" he asked.

"Yes. You aren't?"

"In bed? No, I'm not insane."

"Didn't you traverse Sadie's desert, cross the Dividing Wall, and fight a Behemoth in hopes of getting the Dagger?"

"After having just met, didn't you beg me to marry you?"

She used her heel to kick his shin. "First of all, I didn't beg for you to marry me. I offered it, as an option."

"Ah, I see. And second?"

"Second, I don't believe you proved you're not insane."

"Apologies."

"Had you chosen to marry me, though, is this what I would've had to deal with? You bemoaning the state of the blankets, and making fun of my stockings?"

He laughed. "No, Gwenivere. Not every night at least."

The sound of her name from him, low and deep and soft, sent shivers down her spine.

"You said we should sleep," he whispered.

"And yet you aren't sleeping."

"I feel inclined to inform you that you aren't, either."

"A shrewd observation. Can you take a guess as to why?"

"Because it's almost your sacrificing hours?"

She took her turn to laugh. It wasn't very funny, but she was finding she was, indeed, exhausted, and the statement caught her off guard.

"The moon isn't full enough for that, unfortunately."

"Hm. A different reason, then."

"Yes, a different one. Ultimately unimportant, though."

She closed her eyes, finding that, although he'd slowly *vanished* his element, the heat of his body, still tucked firmly against hers, kept her warm.

"Unimportant?" he asked, after a moment of silence.

"In the grand scheme of life, yes."

"And in the grand scheme of your life, specifically?"

She brought her hand to his, lacing her fingers through it before answering, "I suppose, in the grand scheme of my life, specifically, it's something of ever-increasing importance."

She felt his smile at the nape of her neck.

"Goodnight, Gwenivere."

He rested his forehead against crown of her hair.

"Goodnight, Dietrich."

CHAPTER FIFTY-FIVE
RYNARA

Rynara woke to a knocking at the door.
    No, not a knocking at the door.
    A knocking at *her* door.
Across the hall.

Someone was knocking at her door across the hall.

Dietrich was still asleep beside her. She was entangled with him, his back flat on the bed, one arm around her, the other at his side. She'd ended up tucked against his chest, curled up and comfortable.

She sat up, praying to the Light the person knocking wasn't Garron.

If he sees Dietrich, he'll kill him, she thought, frantically jumping from the bed. Dietrich finally stirred. For all the tension that usually held him at night, he seemed completely relaxed now.

Not wanting to miss a potentially important message, Rynara ignored him as he rubbed his eyes and sat up. She sprinted to the door, opening and closing it hurriedly as she stepped into the hall.

Teniv was there. The big woman turned at the noise, noticed it was her, then looked back and forth between the rooms.

"You switched?" she asked.

Before Rynara could answer, Dietrich opened his door.

Just be glad it's not Garron. Just be glad it's not Garron. Just be glad it's not Garron.

Teniv's eyes widened at the surprise of another person walking out. They widened further when they realized who the person was.

"Hello again," the woman said, collecting herself. She lifted her chin and crossed her arms, showing off impressive muscles.

Maybe Rynara did wish it was Garron.

"Hello, Madam Teniv," Dietrich said. Rynara refused to turn and look at him, but given how quickly he'd followed her out, she had to guess he still wasn't wearing a shirt.

She hoped her body in front of his at least covered his strange scars.

Or that he had the common sense to cover them with his hands.

"I didn't realize there was a new initiation process," Teniv said. Her words were for Rynara, but her hooded eyes stayed locked on Dietrich.

"We were researching ways into . . . where we wished to go," Rynara said. She wished she'd thought to put on trousers. Or a different shirt. She wished she wasn't obviously wearing Dietrich's shirt, which hung on her like a nightgown.

My hair is likely a mess too, she thought, fighting the urge to pat it down.

"Might we discuss things inside?" she offered, gesturing to her room. "I'll just need to get my key."

Teniv didn't answer. She flexed her arms, her eyes boring into Dietrich.

Rynara could only imagine he was meeting Teniv's terrifying glare with a honey-filled smirk.

"I'm going to get my key," she said. She turned around and shoved past Dietrich, then snatched her clothes from the floor, then her boots, then her tossed-aside stockings, which she'd eventually agreed to take off, begrudgingly admitting at some point that the sheets felt far better on her bare feet. When she'd grabbed all her clothes, she pulled her key from her vest pocket and ran back to the hall.

Teniv and Dietrich were still standing as they'd been; her expression hadn't changed, and his, when Rynara finally glanced at him, was exactly as she'd predicted.

"The book I marked is on the table," she said. "Let me know later if there's anything there that could help."

"Will do." His voice was lower than normal and rough from sleep. The sound made something stir inside her, but she couldn't let herself react. She didn't want to pour salt in the wound that was bloody and exposed to Teniv.

Without saying a word, Rynara opened her door and hurried Teniv in.

She expected the woman to scold her. Instead, once they were alone, she found Teniv nodding in approval.

"A warrior," she said. "I knew you had fine taste."

"That wasn't what it looked like."

"You didn't fall asleep in his rooms semi-naked?"

Rynara clutched her bundle of clothes tighter.

"It's not *exactly* what it looked like."

Teniv laughed. "I don't care what—or who—you do in your spare time."

She ducked when Rynara tossed a stocking at her.

They were both grinning.

"He's knowledgeable on poisons," Rynara explained. "I've been working with him to see if there's something we could use to get into the Sanctuary. Last night, I just happened to fall asleep there."

"Just last night, hm?"

Teniv made a show of bending her body and looking around Rynara. The bed behind her was made, and clearly hadn't been slept in for weeks.

"I've been working with him a lot."

Teniv righted. "You've seemed happier these last few weeks."

"Did you have a message for me?" Rynara asked, trying to refocus. "I heard your knocking. It sounded urgent."

"The new recruits aren't ready," Teniv answered, matter-of-factly. "Unless you and the plate of breakfast have a poison ready, then we either inform the enforcers, and leave it up to them, or we get Luthier in."

Rynara quirked a brow. "Plate of breakfast?"

"It's the best meal."

"And if I tell him you said that?"

"Don't do that. It'll inflate his ego."

Rynara snorted. "I'm not sure that's possible."

She sat down on the edge of her bed. Before, she'd thought her and Dietrich's rooms were identical, but she saw now, sitting comfortably against the thick, unused blanket, that her bed didn't have the same frame. There were no railings at the foot or anything to hold on to at the head.

Focus. She needed to focus.

"Not the enforcers," she said, crossing one leg atop the other. "We send someone in. Not Luthier, though, anyone else—"

"It has to be Luthier."

Rynara glowered. "There are others. The three of us are not the only Westerners in the group."

"Do you trust anyone else as much?"

She sighed, not wanting to concede the point, but quietly answered, "No."

"Is there anyone else who's as calm and even-keeled as he is?"

Rynara thought about the other trusted Hawks. Antigone came to mind, with her smattering of freckles. The woman's near constant stream of energy and too innocent spirit would likely be crushed as a slave within the Sanctuary.

The other Westerners were all somewhat similar to Antigone. They were strips of fabric cut from the same cloth. Different keys, but the same song.

None of them would do as well as Garron

"No," Rynara admitted reluctantly. "There aren't."

Teniv walked over and sat on the bed. Her muscular frame and bulk made it dip noticeably in her direction. In the morning light, the burn scars on her neck shone.

"I know you love him," she said. "And trust me, I understand why. He's among the best of men. There was a reason he went from being Luthier to Garron Hillborne, the great Golden Knight of Xenith. He's selfless and good. He's the kind of man you want to believe the heroes we've heard about in stories are actually like. If kings were like him, we wouldn't have masquerades and gatherings celebrating peace, because peace is all we'd know."

Teniv placed a hand on Rynara's arm, rubbing in consolingly.

"But he's not a king. He's a soldier. And he's a damn good one. If you're going to lead this group, you can't treat the rest of the Hawks like fodder, and him like like a pampered prince."

The older woman couldn't possibly have known, but with

her brief speech, she'd revealed to Rynara that she'd done to Garron what Gerard had done to her.

She'd undergone so much training throughout her life, and still her father had thought it best to keep her confined. He'd deemed her too delicate for the cruelties of the world, too inexperienced to attend trade deals. When she'd eventually reign, he thought she'd need a husband to protect her.

She was free from the cage, now. She was putting her skills to use, and, with the support of her Hawks, and Teniv and Luthier, and Dietrich too, she was starting to find her footing. The shoes she walked in weren't as fine. The rooms she slept in weren't as large. There were prices to her freedom, but they were prices she'd pay again and again if it meant she could finally serve the home she loved.

I can't take that away from Garron, she thought. *He can't have sacrificed everything to serve me, only to be kept to the side.*

"If he's truly fine with this plan," Rynara said, grabbing Teniv's hand and holding it, "then we'll go through with it."

Teniv's smiled. "That's a fine decision. I'll let him and the Hawks know."

She rose to leave, hands resting on her knees as she muttered something about getting older and not being as spry as she used to be. When she stood fully, and yawned loudly, she turned back to Rynara, touching the blunt ends of her hair.

"Did you know you let it go back to red?" she asked.

Rynara instinctively grabbed her hair. It rested just above her shoulder. She'd cut and dyed it when she'd left the palace, knowing trackers would be searching for the royal red waves. She'd cut and dyed it many times since then, but recently she'd stopped using the dye, letting the baths she'd taken slowly rinse it out. When she walked about the city now, she wrapped her head, noting that many of the Easterners in Sarabai did the same, and even some Westerners who'd adopted the Sadiyan style.

"I know," she answered, smiling. "I suppose I wanted to be more like the Phoenix everyone calls me."

Teniv smiled back, dropping her hair. "Seems more like Gwenivere Verigrad than the Phoenix."

It wasn't a scolding statement. If anything, it was said with a motherly pride.

Making sure there were no other things to report, Teniv gave a small salute, walked to the door, and bid Rynara a good day.

CHAPTER FIFTY-SIX
DIETRICH

The decision was final. If Dietrich couldn't find a poison to use against the Sanctuary, Gwenivere's knight was going in.

She slept even less than she had before, which meant that he too was sleeping less. Both of them often fell asleep on the floor, books in hand, trying to find helpful information.

The swamps she'd told him about had seemed promising, until he discovered that they were out in the Far West, a place well beyond Xenith and its neighbors, and with international tension, it likely wouldn't be possible to ship anything in. Even if it was, it wouldn't arrive in time, and it would cost them an enormous fortune. Teniv seemed to have deep pockets, but it would still be an exorbitant expense.

His lack of sleep was making words jumble together when he tried to read. He drank a lot of sundrops, but the drink couldn't keep him from writing nonsense in his notes, things that became indiscernible mere hours later. When he tried to pour liquids from one vial into the other, he found he rarely did so without dripping some onto himself, accumulating new scars.

Gwenivere was the only thing that could make him sleep. When she'd decided he'd done enough—or when she herself was too tired to continue—she bid him rest. She'd wrap his injured fingers, then beckon him to the bed.

He wanted to find answers for her, but the thought of sleep was always too sweet a temptation to resist. Especially when it was accompanied by her, wearing his clothes, and folding herself comfortably against him.

Now it was the last night. He expected they'd both be up until the morning, likely not sleeping at all, but instead, she decided to retire early and pulled him away from his desk.

"You can stop," she said quietly. The lights in the room had been recharged by the inn's staff a few nights before, specifically the woman Dietrich had grumbled hello to the morning he'd gone to the Sanctuary. Gwenivere walked to each lamp, turning them down to nothing, leaving only the fire to light the room.

"It's the last night," he countered, writing something in his notes. He'd had to hide them and all his vials when the woman had come in, but it'd been worth it to have the lamplight stronger and his eyes not ache from the strain of reading in the dark.

"I know," she said. She sounded resigned. "You did what you could. We need to commit to the other path now."

Dietrich turned, facing her. He expected to see her angry, or at least attempting—and failing—to suppress her anger, but instead, she seemed resolute.

At no point had she stopped believing they could find a solution, but now that they hadn't, she seemed at peace.

He brushed a hand through his hair.

"I'm close," he said. "I really think—"

"Dietrich." She closed the distance between them. She put her hands against his vest, and he forced himself to take steady breaths as she began undoing its buttons.

The result wouldn't be any different than it had been the last few days. They always ended up in his bed, worn out and deprived of sleep, each wearing whatever they deemed finest for rest. Still, something about her rasped voice, tranquil and a touch hoarse, along with it being *her* fingers slowly undoing the buttons, made him dizzy.

"Are you close enough that you could have this done, with absolute certainty it wouldn't kill anyone we're hoping to save?"

The words weren't admonishment. They weren't spoken harshly. He expected them to still wound him, to force him to accept he'd failed.

Instead, they gave him permission to forgive that he had.

"You can't know how much I've appreciated this," she said, forcing his vest off. "All the effort you've put into trying to keep Garron safe."

He dropped his shoulders, letting the vest fall to his hand. She took it from him carefully, knowing he had dangerous things placed within its pockets, and draped it over the back of a chair.

"If ever I meet *your* Garron," she said, returning to him, her fingers now starting on the buttons of his shirt. "If I ever meet Culter, I'll do anything I can to repay this kindness and help him in any trials he might face."

Dietrich settled against his desk, hands clutching tightly to its edge.

"Do you remember what I said, about people not knowing my name?"

She paused, turquoise eyes meeting his.

"I told you how it made me feel like no one ever really

knew me. I'd only thought about myself in that scenario; I hadn't realized that part of what was missing was having someone acknowledge the other people in my life."

He bit the inside of his cheek, unsure whether he was speaking clearly.

What she'd said was important. Meaningful.

He wanted her to know that, he was just so . . . tired. It was hard to think straight.

"I don't think I'm making sense," he said, pressing his fingers into his forehead. Her hands, he noticed, still hadn't moved from his chest.

"I think I understand," she said, finally continuing to unbutton the rest of his shirt. "When people only knew the false you, that was all you could ever be. When people know you for who you really are, that includes *the people* who make you who you really are. Your friends, your family. . . ." Her fingers pushed his shirt open, finding the scars on his stomach.

His grip on the desk tightened.

"Whatever else you love," she finished. She pushed gently, and he acquiesced, letting her slip the shirt from his shoulders. She buttoned it back up, then folded it neatly, setting it on the seat of the chair his vest rested on.

Once she'd done that, she turned from him and began undressing.

He thought to look away. He'd always looked away before, the few times she didn't put one of his shirts on first, but something between them seemed different tonight. There was a wall that'd stood between them before, something tall and intimidating but easily dismantled, once they'd begun removing the stones. There seemed fewer barriers, now, fewer borders or lines that weren't meant to be crossed.

Some still existed. He'd only really known her for a short time, and she him, but that time had seemed like finally breathing clean air when he'd been trapped within a sandstorm.

As she tossed her own vest on the chair she usually sat in, he made out her silhouette through the light of the fire. When her shirt followed, he saw the lean muscles of her back, and the definition of her arms, the hours and weeks and years she'd spent mastering blades and bows and daggers.

There was a cloth tied around her arm, one he assumed hid her Amulet. She fingered at it, a thing he'd noticed her do when she was nervous, or anxious, or lost in thought.

She kept the wrapping that held her breasts tight as she took his shirt—a different one than what she'd just removed—and placed it over her head. Her hair was still too short to need to pull it free from the shirt's collar as it fell over her, but it was long enough to sit oddly after the static had caught it and cast it in different directions.

Not sure what compelled him, he crossed the room to her, thinking to pat her hair down. Instead, he found his arms circling her. She sucked in a breath, then settled, resting her head back against his chest and her hands against his own.

"I'm sorry I couldn't find something," he said. "I know tomorrow will be difficult for you. Whatever you wish to do, I'll join you."

When she didn't say anything, he added, "You think sparring is relaxing. Perhaps we can do that."

She smiled. He brushed her hair to the side, wanting to see it.

"When is it happening?" he asked. "How . . . how is it happening?"

She took a heavy breath. He let her gather her thoughts. He knew it was challenging for her—even if she'd accepted the plan—to let the person she loved the most risk his life.

"Early tomorrow morning," she said. "Or tonight,

depending on how you look at it. There's a place called Jezalee. One of the Hawks we have working for the enforcers says she heard Redeemers are meeting there to pass contraband along. Garron is going to be 'in the wrong place at the wrong time.' When they spot him, we're hoping the Redeemers will take him peacefully and bring him back to the Sanctuary. A lot of previous kidnappings happened that way. The Redeemers don't seem to want any witnesses revealing their hideouts or trading spots."

Dietrich nodded, holding her tighter.

"I will let Seera know," he said. "I imagine you have Hawks that'll be watching to make sure it goes according to plan, but once they actually get to the caves, Seera can let me know if anything goes awry."

"Thank you," she whispered, clinging to him. There was pain in her voice.

Gently, Dietrich turned her to face him. She kept her arms where they'd been, firmly held together at her stomach. Her face dipped down. She was afraid, it seemed, to let him see the tears in her eyes.

How bizarre, that she could be so strong when comforting others, only to be so ashamed when she needed comfort herself.

He knew she'd loved her father, but it angered him that the man who was supposed to have made her feel safest had forced her inward. He'd made her believe she could only show anger, frustration, or strength.

Though she looked away, Dietrich felt it miraculous that she'd come to trust him enough to stay nearby when her vulnerability surfaced. She didn't change the subject anymore or push the emotions down. She didn't storm off or shove him away or return to her rooms. Defying all she'd been taught, she let herself be small. Sad. Uncertain.

He lifted her chin, wiping away her tears. Her nose was red. Her eyes were red too, the tears making their turquoise color almost green. The crying was a quiet thing, unlike the sobs she'd released weeks before, but it was a picture of her pain, nonetheless. He folded his arms around her again, finding even this motion between them had changed.

She was usually reluctant when he comforted.

Now, she didn't resist having her pain acknowledged.

"Come on," he said, pulling away and rubbing her arms. "Let's go to sleep."

She nodded, and they parted ways as they each went to their unclaimed yet understood sides of the bed. Before she settled in, she slipped out of her leggings, then quickly hurried into the warmth of the bed and the welcome of his embrace.

Dietrich felt more of her tears fall against his chest. He didn't say anything, only settling one arm around her, the other stroking her hair. She'd been letting it go back to red, he'd realized, the color almost pink as it escaped the blonde. He was quite fond of the shade, and he found the thought of it returning completely red strangely exciting.

"What is Culter like?" she whispered.

He took a breath and laughed, the first thing coming to mind being all the lewd songs the watchman had taught him. Gwenivere looked up, smiling when he kept laughing. He waved his hand in apology, then wiped at his face, forcing his expression to reset.

"He's like a puppy," he said. "He's very excited about things. He seems oblivious sometimes, like he doesn't realize why everyone seems so amused by him.

"His humor is that of a child. He's nearing his sixth decade, and he still laughs anytime he hears a story involving farts.

"He treats every woman with the utmost respect. He used to teach me songs no boy should sing, then listen to me sing them in front of my brother just to see how confused he'd get by the lyrics."

He remembered that last look Culter had given him, the look of horror, and despair. He fought against a shudder. He'd hated that so quickly after he'd been reunited with his mentor, he'd brought him such pain.

"He sounds delightful," Gwenivere said. Dietrich agreed, noting the way her fingers had almost imperceptibly begun brushing against his chest, rather than simply resting there.

He let his head settle again hers.

"And Garron?" he asked. "What was it like, having the mythical knight as your personal guard?"

"Not as fun as Culter," she said, smiling. "Growing up, he was the perfect knight: loyal, collected, protective. He has an infinite amount of patience. He's quiet, but when he does talk, you can't help but listen.

"He's a wealth of wisdom and kindness, but he's also the strongest person I know. He's endured a lot in his life, yet he's never allowed his pain to seep onto others."

She moved her arm until it wrapped around his torso.

"He's my favorite person in the world."

Dietrich kissed the top of her head.

"Then he's one of mine too."

Gwenivere pressed herself up, her weight leaning against him. He let his hand find hers before meeting her gaze.

Seera, he thought, opening his mind. He told her quickly of the planned kidnapping, and she confirmed she'd look out for the knight.

"Seera's too," he added. "She's going to look after him."

Gwenivere continued to stare at him, wordless.

It was unnerving.

"We should sleep," he told her. "As best we can, anyway. I'll listen for any news from Seera."

Gwenivere nodded. He felt he could breathe again when she blinked and returned to settling her head against his chest.

He kissed the top of her head one more time before pulling the blankets up and covering them both.

Six hours later, Garron was caught. Everything had gone according to plan. The knight wasn't hurt. He'd been pretending to be drunk, so the Redeemers were a little rough with him, but only because he was large, not because they were hurting him unnecessarily.

Seera relayed the news to him, her body hidden within the cliffs, but her ears and eyes listened and watched as the Redeemers made their way to the caves.

Dietrich let Gwenivere sleep as the updates came, until a single problem with the plan came up.

They're not going to send him to the Sanctuary, Seera said. *Due to his strength, they've decided to send him over the mountains into the Dividing Wall's mines.*

Dietrich jolted awake, shaking Gwenivere. He told her what Seera had said.

She immediately began dressing, dawning her finest element-resistant clothing and gear.

"Tell Teniv!" she ordered. "Her room is—"

"I know which one it is," he said.

They didn't waste time talking or planning. If Garron was brought over the Dividing Wall, he'd officially be in the most prominently held of the Redeemers' lands. With countless mines running up and down the Eastern side of the mountains, they'd lose months, maybe even years, trying to track down which one he'd been brought to.

Dietrich found Teniv's room. Leaving Seera's part in everything out of it, he brought her up to speed. The woman sprang into action, just as he had, then looked around him, searching for Gwenivere.

"Where is she?"

Dietrich turned around, expecting she'd been just behind him.

She wasn't there.

He and Teniv shared a look before running outside. Gwenivere couldn't have gone far. Maybe she was upstairs, equipping herself with more weapons or jotting down commands for Teniv to give the rest of the Hawks.

He ran back in and sprinted up the steps, four at a time. He was back to her rooms in a matter of seconds. When he burst in, spare key in hand, he found the room empty, save for a note sitting on the edge of her bed. He hurried over to it, nearly collapsing as he read.

We have your Phoenix. *Meet us at the Sanctuary in three days' time.*

—*Navar*

CHAPTER FIFTY-SEVEN
X'ODIA

X'odia's cell was made of wood.
It'd been a hastily fashioned thing. Shoddy. Easily destroyed.

Before it'd been built, city watch had been assigned to guard her. People would come to gawk at her, curious of the strange Evean woman with the swirling eyes. Some remembered the messages that'd spread about her the year before, when Markeem and the innkeeper had been killed by Rellor. Murder hadn't run rampant in the city, then. She'd been the most hated person in Riverdee for a few weeks, even though very few had seen her. For those who had remembered that hatred, they'd approached her with stones in hand, ready to enact their revenge.

The guards had managed to keep most of the stones away. She kneeled in the center of them, skirts perpetually wet from the puddles on the ground. There were twelve guards in total assigned to watch her. They didn't complete a full barricade around her. Some of the stones found their marks.

Without the ability to heal, those first few days were agony.

She returned to being separated from her elements. Bruises and cuts marked her temple and arms where the stones landed. One of the guards, the young man named Scavol, applied a healing salve where skin was split, but there was little else she could do. The people around her believed her responsible for the terrors that faced their city, both the murders and the Attack of Fiends. Even Scavol was struck by stones when he got too close.

X'odia thought to escape early. She wished to, but the time wasn't right. When she was ready, she'd come out of the chains. The city would see that she'd suffered, and they would see that she'd triumphed. Navar's manipulation of their faith was a twisted and tangled thing. She sought to undo the threads and set it right.

It occurred to her that it was arrogance, to some degree, that drove her. When she emerged from this penance, the people might truly believe her a product of divinity.

Not might.

Would.

She remembered feeling blasphemous when she'd saved the sailors, all those weeks ago, for letting them think her a sliver of the Creator sent down to help them. She didn't worry about that now. Any tool at her disposal would be used.

Let the people talk, when she had her freedom. If it gave them comfort in the end to make her more than a person, fine.

It would be better than the thing Navar had reduced her to.

After the first few days, the guards left, and it was only the hastily erected cage that held her. She no longer had her elements available to keep people away, as she had when she'd first come to the square. Attempts to harm her would go unimpeded.

The cage was the size of a small shed. Rather than cell bars, there were wood planks of various sizes.

A week into her captivity, someone tried to burn it down.

She'd been tempted to leave, then. When the blaze had first begun, it'd burned through some of the planks, leaving a wide opening in the cage. She'd been completely exposed to whoever might try to come for her. Fortunately, the flames kept fearful passersby away. Two young men had started the fire. She'd watched them light the matches and had heard one of them whisper, *Look how she just watches us—look at her eyes! She's not natural.* They'd run off once the flames had caught.

The heat spread up and around the wood. It licked the edges of each plank. The heat surrounded her, intimidating.

Leave now, it seemed to say. *The people will never believe you innocent.*

Run.

She'd stayed. There was no top to the cage, which, in the end, had likely been what saved her. Smoke had swept into her lungs, but without anything above her to risk collapsing, only the perimeter had burned away. Emergency task force members came before the cage was completely gone, and though some only sat back and watched—likely Redeemers themselves—others rushed in to put the fire out.

Stop this, one of them had urged, grabbing her arm. *Face the Riverdean courts. You'll die out here.*

Navar would buy the courts, she'd said calmly, pulling her arm back. *If I'm to die, I'd rather it be in the light. I don't wish to be murdered in the shadows.*

When the man had stood there, imploring her still, she'd added, *Fear naught, for I will not die. The Creator will grant me the power to break these chains. You will see then that it's the Redeemers who are evil.*

The man had crouched down, kneeling in front of her.

I know he's evil, he'd whispered. *More of Riverdee believes you innocent then you might think.*

Another cage was made.

It was coated with fire-resistance paint.

How many weeks went by after that, X'odia couldn't be sure. She couldn't risk sleeping, not fully, at least, and thus, the days blurred together. She drifted off from time to time, her body unable to renew as it usually did, but the rest came in bursts and blinks. If her theory about her visions proved true, there was a link between them and dreams. When she'd been imprisoned by the Elite, she'd learned the Sight could not claim her while she was in chains, and if it tried, she'd face great pain.

She sat awake as much as she could, then. Always watching. Always on edge.

When night came, she shivered. Her body ached from how hard she shook. Her lips dried and bled when frost came. Her scalp itched. She'd forgone food and drink when she could. It was the only thing Navar's men bothered to bring her, and she'd been afraid of poison when it'd first come, but she knew it would've looked bad for him to have her die by such a cowardly hand.

Her challenge had been to allow the Light to determine her innocence. If he interfered in that, it would only serve to prove her point.

She was ravenous and thirsty, but she forced herself to consume little. It was humiliating enough to be chained and caged like a rabid animal. Relieving herself in front of everyone was not something she wished to become commonplace. As much as possible, she waited until the dark hours of night. Sometimes people were awake then, but they were usually drunkards or young people hurriedly sneaking out to engage in mischief. Her presence had become such a staple in the bell tower plaza that few in those instances paid her mind. She was as much a fixture to them as the bells themselves.

Eventually, a group of mostly men and a few women approached. They appeared in the early hours of the morning, before the sun had risen. They held crude weapons, clubs mostly, and small daggers. X'odia had thought they'd come to kill her. She'd watched them, readying her *auroras* as more and more poured out from the alleys, even knowing the disconnect *calling* would provide.

One of the men advanced toward her. He had weatherworn skin and dark brown eyes. His sleeves were rolled up, revealing inked forearms and wiry muscles.

X'odia fought the instinct to back into the corner of the cage. Whether she was in the center of it or at the edge, it would matter little. If this man wished to harm her, he'd find a way.

"It's her," he grumbled, squinting. He stepped up to the edge of the cage, hand wrapping around one of the smaller planks.

"Do you remember me, lass?"

X'odia shook her head. "I'm sorry. I do not."

"It was dark that night," he said. His voice was as coarse as his appearance. Prianthian, mixed with Mesidian. X'odia had never heard such an accent.

"Enlighten me, good man," she said. Her own voice was hoarse from disuse. Her throat ached from the effort, and her dried lips cracked. "I don't wish to offend."

He crouched down and offered her a smile. It was astounding how it completely altered his face.

"You saved me and me crew," he said. "I carried you back to an inn after."

"The ship," she managed. "The one caught out at sea during the storm."

"You were the Light come to life," he said. "You saved us. Why?"

X'odia swallowed and shrugged. "Because I could."

The answer seemed to satisfy him. He nodded approvingly, then stood, back resting against the planks.

"We can do the same for you now," he said.

No one tried to throw things or burn the cage down after that.

Sailors were highly respected in Riverdee. Each time someone came to the plaza and began arguing with the ones now guarding X'odia, others would join in, more often than not on the side of the sailors. They were the lifeblood of the city, after all. Sea trade and ocean cuisine were staples. To have the sailors defend X'odia was like having priests offer blessings.

The story of their miraculous voyage and her courage in saving them began to spread.

They took turns protecting her cage. X'odia discovered they spent their off time going around the city, tearing down any posts that spoke poorly of her. They put up their own in their place, the drawings and stories as crudely done as their weapons. They'd shown her a few once, handing them through the cage bars. She'd smiled, appreciating the gallant way they had depicted her, though sometimes their penmanship had been difficult to decipher.

Azgar, their leader, spoke little. He offered to cut the cage down and help her escape, and though the offer was tempting, she refused.

"The storm," she said. "It will be my deliverance."

He seemed skeptical but didn't argue. She was a piece of divinity in his eyes, after all. He accepted that whatever she said would come to pass, would.

Days later—how many later, X'odia didn't know—a Mesidian woman came. She asked the sailors if she could speak to 'the captive,' as if they were her jailors. They searched her for weapons, patting her down, and when they found none, they allowed her closer.

"Hello," the woman said. She seemed nervous and timid, but her eyes were a clear blue and steadfast. X'odia leaned forward. She knew she smelled, so she didn't want to get too close.

"Hello," she said. "My name is X'odia."

"I know your name," the woman said. She pulled her cloak's hood tight over her head. It was raining today, a light drizzle but strong enough to hurt if the raindrops landed in one's eyes.

"From the printings?" X'odia asked.

"No. From these."

The woman pulled out a few parchments from a satchel at her side. She didn't hand them over and, likely due to the rain, swiftly placed them back in the satchel, but not before X'odia caught handwritten words.

Not printings. Letters.

"My husband's name was Markeem," the woman said. "He was one of the Elite."

X'odia perked up. "Your husband was very kind. He gave me hope when I was imprisoned before."

Droplets clung to the woman's lashes. They spilled down

her cheek, and X'odia wondered if it was only the rain, or if tears had joined them.

"How did he die?" she whispered. "They told me you killed him. I use to get his letters all the time. Then I got a letter that he was dead. He never got to meet our child."

The woman's lips quivered. X'odia wanted to reach out to her, to hold her, but of course, the cage separated them, and she didn't know if the woman would believe her testimony.

"I was imprisoned outside of the city, in an abandoned shack," X'odia said. "When I was brought here, into the city itself, Dravian Valcor's Elite joined again with Odin's. Most of the soldiers got drunk that night. Markeem kept watch over me in one of the rooms. He didn't partake in the drinking or whoring.

"I awoke that night to Rellor Bordinsua attempting to rape me. When I escaped, I saw Markeem dead in the room's chair."

Everything X'odia said was true, but laying it out so bluntly made her feel cold and callous.

"Rellor killed him," she said. "He was wild. He didn't seem like he cared for anything but inflicting pain, but I do think he reserved that for me. For your husband . . . I think his death was quick."

The woman nodded. X'odia had no idea whether she believed her, but she walked away, not bothering to give parting words.

X'odia watched her go. She'd care for that woman, if she could. Riverdee and its crises may have been at the forefront of X'odia's thoughts, but she knew vaguely of what'd happened after Dravian's men were killed. She'd had to know, given how attached Roland was to it all.

Markeem's death would've brought coin to the woman from the crown, as recompense, if the crown still stood. X'odia hoped she had family or friends to help give her shelter and partake in the raising of her child.

"Was all that true?" Azgar asked. "The Elite really did that to you?"

"Yes." X'odia folded her legs beneath her. "Rellor Bordinsua did. Markeem, that woman's husband, was very sweet. Dravian Valcor was perhaps not kind, but he treated me like a person. He believed me innocent right away, but his orders were to keep me imprisoned. I think it weighed on him."

Azgar replied with a grunt.

"You don't believe me?"

"No, I believe you. I just think you must be a bit dull in the head, to take pity on your captors."

"I took no pity on Rellor," she said. "He was less than a rat."

"What happened to him?"

"Dravian cut off his head."

Azgar nodded. "Good man that."

"For decapitating his fellow general?"

"For decapitating a monster."

After a moment, Azgar lit some kind of large, soft stick, blowing smoke from his mouth as it burned.

"I take it back," he said, holding his hand over the stick to keep the rain from putting it out. "I can see why you'd not hate the man who you saw do some good by you. I don't think any of them were good, though, not even that Markeem. A good man would've defied his king and set you free from the start."

X'odia didn't argue with him.

She wasn't sure she disagreed.

"The storm's coming tonight," Azgar said, changing the topic. He shielded his head from the rain and looked up. "It won't be as bad as the one we were caught in, but it'll be close. We'll guard you for as long as we can, but I'm not asking my crew to sit out here and risk death."

"You've risked yourselves enough," X'odia said. "I'm in your debt."

"No, you're not. Our lives are yours. You ever need anything, just ask, and we'll see that you get it."

X'odia smiled. "Thank you."

"You ready for your reckoning?" he asked. "Your cleansing or whatever it is you're waiting for?"

"I'm ready to be out of the cage."

"We could get you out now. You don't have to go through with this."

"No, that won't be necessary. Though . . . when the storm starts to die down, might I ask a favor?"

"Depends."

"It'll make you very rich."

"Definitely, then."

She chuckled.

"Where will I find you all? Is there somewhere you'll all be?"

He gave her the place they planned to stay in, and the directions to it from the plaza.

"Perfect. I will see you when the storm begins to die."

He glanced back at her, brow raised, smoke stick pressed between his lips.

"Whatever you say. You have any wishes before that?"

X'odia was about to say no, then smiled.

"Make sure there are writers watching my cage tonight, through their windows. I want to make sure everyone knows it wasn't any of you who set me free. Pay them what you have to—I'll make sure you're compensated. I also could use a new pair of clothes and a hot meal if you can spare it."

"I'll get you the finest of both things, Lady X'odia."

CHAPTER FIFTY-EIGHT
X'ODIA

The storm would arrive around midnight. Even without Azgar's warning, the city made it clear what was coming. The bells rang their ominous tones. People boarded up windows. When X'odia listened to the conversations of passersby, she caught scared whispers.

The roof hasn't been repaired fully since the last storm.
Father refuses to leave his house.
I don't know what to do with the horses.

She felt sympathy for them after seeing the carnage of the last storm, but she had her own fears. If all transpired as she hoped, she would emerge from her cage unchained, healed, and prepared to finally destroy Navar's stronghold.

Just as the storm clouds began to roll through, one last person came to see her.

Zuri.

"I told you not to come," X'odia said, patting down her clothes. Azgar had indeed found her the finest of garb; thick black pants that tucked into sturdy boots, and a long, sleeveless overcoat to keep her warm. It tied in the back, and was lined with wool and scales. She'd needed something that could be laced up, as she couldn't get the clothing on with the shackles still tight around her wrists, so her current shirt remained beneath everything else. The sailors had all stood shoulder to shoulder along the cage as one of them reached around the planks and helped her get her old clothes off, and her new clothes on.

One of them, a sailor with long hair, had insisted X'odia scoot to the cage's edge so they could redo her braids. The last bit of her ensemble was a few pieces of armor, some lining her arms like blades, others strapped to her thighs and shoulders, and atop her head, she wore what looked like half a helmet. She couldn't see what she looked like, but she thought that if she could, she too might believe herself a piece of the divine.

"I had to come," Zuri said, eyeing her garb. Her friend looked at her with a mix of awe and concern, her hazel eyes wide and her forehead pinched.

"I didn't want you to see me like this." X'odia reached through the cage. Besides eating and changing, she'd also managed to scrub as much of herself clean as she could while her clothes had been off. She didn't feel bad now, drawing close and clasping her friend's hands.

"Roland keeps asking for you," Zuri said.

"You didn't tell him I was here, did you?"

"I told him you've been trying to gather information."

X'odia breathed a sigh of relief. Above her, thunder rumbled.

"How is he?"

"He's . . . he's getting better. He has an addiction to Root. Not as bad as Cara's, but still."

"How did the Redeemers force him to take it?"

Zuri met her eyes. Though X'odia had been the one

comforting her, Zuri's fingers seemed to twist, until it was her hands covering X'odia's own.

"They didn't," she said. "Roland's been taking Root since before the fire. He got it off Dar and Callum."

X'odia's heart sank. She closed her eyes, resting her forehead on the wood in front of her.

All the signs had been right there. His skin had lost its color. His hair had looked thinner. His body, once strong and stocky, had started to look lean.

I even thought he resembled Cara a bit, she thought.

How had she not seen the depths of her friend's suffering?

"You swear he's doing better?" she asked, looking back to Zuri. "He's not taking it anymore?"

"He's not," she insisted. "And yes, he's getting better. It'll take a long time, not just to get better from this but to help him through what pushed him down this path in the first place. It's like hunger, for him, or thirst."

"Tell him I'll see him soon," X'odia said. She had tears in her eyes. "Tell him I love him and I miss him. Make sure he knows that."

"I will," Zuri said. She kissed X'odia's hands. "You'll tell him yourself, though, next time you see him."

She said goodbye, and walked away.

A part of X'odia wanted her to stay. A part of her wanted someone she loved and trusted beside her as she battled the storm, but this was something she needed to do on her own. No one could help her.

The people of Riverdee had seen her suffer enough, though. It was time now for them to see her triumph.

Darkness came. The moon, full and bright, was eclipsed by the clouds. Stars winked out of sight. Torchlight died. The wind screamed its warning.

The storm had arrived.

Now was the time. Alone, and deeply, deeply afraid, X'odia closed her eyes, took a deep breath, and began *calling* ice.

The storm bellowed. The sky mocked her.

Look how I wield air and water and wind, it seemed to say. *Look how naturally it bends to my will, when you can't even touch it.*

The shackles around her wrists began to glow as they absorbed the element. X'odia ground her teeth but kept *calling*.

Needles pricked at her skin. Her heart and head seemed like they might burst. Enormous pressure built just behind her eyes, and every muscle in her body grew weak.

She collapsed to the ground, sweating. The shackles continued to glow, though the blue-white color began to slowly dim. Before it was completely gone, X'odia rose to her feet, held her hands out in front of her, and *called* again.

Pain. More pain. So much more pain. Her elements were right there in her mind, just out of reach. An invisible barrier blocked them, and each time the lights came up to it, it was as if the entire world came crashing down against her. No one was beside her, but it seemed as if an army was stabbing her with spears and piercing her with arrows.

She collapsed again.

No, she thought, seeing lightning spread across the sky. Thunder came next, shaking the ground around her.

No!

She rose a third time and *called* again.

The shackles grew brighter. The more she hurt, the more they glowed.

Some of the lights were getting through. Cracks were forming in the wall.

The shackles were beginning to grow cold.

If you try to call *elements, the chains drain them.*

Roland's voice, from weeks ago.

If you try calling them enough, eventually the shackles will fill, and release the elements back out.

Usually it kills the person chained.

Usually.

Usually, but not always.

And X'odia was no ordinary person.

What might've taken another person months, even years to *call* forth, X'odia could *call* in moments. If the chains released all of that at once, in a single explosion, much would be destroyed from the impact.

Fire would burn.

Lightning would electrocute.

Earth would shatter.

Water would drown.

Ice, though?

Ice would sever.

X'odia kept *calling*. The storm kept raging. The worst of it was nearing, its winds whipping across her skin, pushing her, forcing her to her knees.

I bow to you now, she thought, screaming as she *called* more ice. *But you and I will rise together.*

With one last burst, X'odia called every white *aurora* in her mind.

The chains shattered.

The wall fell.

Shards of ice shot out.

They stabbed into her stomach. Her thighs. Her chest. They punctured her lungs.

She fought to breath.

Blood rushed from her wounds. Spilled out beneath her ribs.

She collapsed again. Choking, she looked to where the chains had been.

Her hands were gone.

It was pain unlike any she'd ever known. She thought of Rellor then, of all he'd inflicted upon her body. She thought of the months in the shack, cold and weary and broken, only wanting food or a kind person to talk to.

Her soul had been broken. Her faith had been shattered. Her body had been mangled and beaten and defiled.

Coughing up blood, X'odia prayed. She still believed in something. Her heart still yearned for a comforting hand, a peace at the end of her life. If that end was now, then she'd done what she could to defy that which was malevolent and wicked. If it wasn't, then she begged to be healed.

Her sight began to blur. Water poured from the sky.

The bells rang.

As X'odia slipped in darkness, she wondered if any bells would ring for her when they found her body.

No, she thought.

I'm not going to die.

Not yet.

Not here.

Not now.

She laid against cold stones. It was peculiar, to have the malleability of water meeting her from above while something hard and unmoving met her from below.

Get up, she told herself. *You've hurt before. You've always healed.*

Get up.

Without her hands, X'odia relied on her core to hoist her from the ground. She shouted at the effort, the wounds in her stomach still open, but whatever damage had been done inside her was healing.

Do you feel that? she asked herself. *Do you feel your lungs filling with air?*

She took a deep breath. She relished the expansion within her as she did.

Look at your wrists, she commanded. *Look.*

The skin grows back. The bones grow back.

She leaned against the planks, sobbing loudly. She was in shock. Her mind, her muscles, her spirit. Everything was in a state of submission, so she sobbed to remind herself that she was alive and that she could still feel everything.

Without a roof over the cage, water continued to rain down on her. The wood itself, while not sturdy, did help break some of the wind. Her back took the torrent. The strength of her thighs fought back against it, keeping her upright.

With the eye of the storm still leagues away, the tips of her fingers had finished forming. Nails rested on them, clean and long. No callouses rested on her palms.

The pain had gone.

Now we join together, she thought, looking up to the sky. She didn't know if it was nature she called to or the Light or the elements in her mind that once again shone brightly. Maybe it was something else. Maybe it was everything.

Pulling herself up, she walked to the center of the cage, *called* air, and pressed.

The wood fell to the ground. X'odia stepped out and made her way to the rest of Navar's storerooms.

CHAPTER FIFTY-NINE
THE BELLS OF RIVERDEE

When the sun broke through the clouds and the dawn had come anew, the people of Riverdee emerged.

They expected to find destruction. There was some. Roofs had caved. Poorly boarded windows had broken. Leaks had led to flooding, ruining possessions.

No one had died, though. Not even the animals.

Throughout the night, a specter had appeared, reached out her hand, and guided people to safety.

When morning comes, she'd commanded, *return to the plaza with ten bells. I will be there.*

The people who'd been saved did as told. First in trickles. Then in waves.

Others came too. The ten-belled square was where announcements were made, after all. Emergency task forces would notify them of where the worst damage was, and the city would rush out to rebuild.

Today, the task force wasn't there.

X'odia was, dressed in finery, sitting on a pile of trunks, gold, and riches.

"The Light has found me innocent," she said. "It revealed to me all the treachery of Navar and his Redeemers. It showed me where to find his stolen wealth, his contraband, and the cures he's kept from you. It guided my feet so I might find the gold he'd used to bribe the city watch, the judges, and the councillors. It exposed to me the poisons he's inflicted upon your sons and daughters and the weapons he's held to their throats.

"If you are in need, come now. I will give to you what you require. This city will no longer be held by lies and terror. Navar's reign is over. Your city watch will serve to protect you again. *I* will serve to protect you."

All around her, sailors began passing out bags of coin. The city watch came too, some laying down their spears and daggers to help.

Others held them firm, so that if Redeemers came, they'd have to come through them first.

ATOP THE HILLS looking out over the city where larger houses dwelled, an old woman walked outside and checked the damage to her home.

She found a large bag of coins on her doorstep, and a note reading, *Thank you for offering me shelter when the last storm came. Consider this a few tokens of my appreciation.*

A MAN NAMED Cillian was brought to Riverdee's ten-belled square. There was a chest of riches awaiting him.

"For your new inn," an Evean woman said. "May it grant others shelter when the next storm comes."

A ROUGH-LOOKING SAILOR, after much effort, found the woman he'd heard claiming to be the widow of an Elite soldier named Markeem. According to the person he now served, Markeem had been a well-loved and well-respected man.

The widow, after much shock and confusion, accepted the multiple bags of coins that were given to her.

"For you and your child," the sailor said, delivering the message he was meant to convey. "May your husband *drift* in peace."

A GIRL NAMED Cara was brought to an inn. She wouldn't know it, not for a few days at least, but a home waited for her when she recovered, as well as a group of healers who would make sure she was taken care of.

TRAGEDY HAD STRUCK the previous year, where King Pierre's Elite had last stayed. A kind woman of middling years had been killed after checking on a fleeing Evean.

That woman had cared for her family. Twin boys and a daughter.

That woman had loved her husband. A man by the name of Edwin Calbright.

Providing for their children was hard work, and Edwin found this especially true while grieving. Some things had to be let go. Health. A nice home. Favorite pastimes. All that mattered to him was trying to fill the gap that'd been left behind. It was difficult enough that his children no longer had a mother. It would be harder still if they didn't have a decent life because of it.

After the most recent storm, Edwin surveyed the damage to his home. A writer friend who'd printed his story moons ago approached him, carrying a note and a bag that made clinking sounds as it was handed over.

In my greatest time of need, your wife was the only person who tried to make sure I was all right. I will never forget that kindness. I know this won't bring her back, but I hope it will at least make life a little easier for you.

When Edwin opened the bag, he found it filled with more riches than he could earn in a lifetime.

Two city guards were in need of finding: a man named Dar and a man named Callum.

It turned out they'd last been seen weeks before, fleeing from the Dusty Boot, before it'd been set ablaze. Word had been announced that there was a reward for anyone who had information on them.

Scavol knew where they were. He'd been the one to free them. They'd been resistant to speak of Navar and the murder victims and the contraband that'd been running through the city.

Your families will be cared for if you confess, Scavol told them. *I think you should take the offer. Especially now that Navar is gone.*

They gave their confession. It listed all the people who'd been killed under Navar's orders.

One had been a woman whose body had been discovered in an alley near the Dusty Boot. Her family had wondered often about her death. It brought them . . . not peace, perhaps, but the beginnings of it, to have some answers regarding her murder.

They were also grateful to know that a young man, an unknown hero who worked at the nearby inn, had been there with her when she'd died. She'd not had to take her last breaths alone.

Riverdee, despite being the essence of Abra'am, had no control over international happenings. It certainly didn't have a say in the trials of foreigners. It was a surprise, then, when a contact between Riverdee's courts and the Arctic's prisons was given a note, insisting a case needed to be reopened.

The case was for a Sadiyan man. He'd killed someone; the note was not trying to deny that. But he'd killed someone to defend his sister. It'd been self-defense on her behalf.

He also had children. Their grandfather was looking after them.

The note urged that even if the man couldn't be set free, he at least deserved to have his sentence lessened.

Across Riverdee, where criminals were kept, nearly seventy Redeemers were bound and left in front of gaols and prisons. The ropes that held them were tied in knots only sailors could make, and the ropes themselves were made of materials not unlike that which lay in element chains.

There weren't enough cells for them, as the continent was in the depths of winter and the roads to the Arctic's prisons were snowed in. Fortunately, many inside the gaols and prisons were innocent, and their sentences would've shown that months ago, if corruption hadn't interfered.

That corruption lay at the feet of each gaol and each prison now. The innocent could be released and room could be made for the guilty.

Rumors said many of the innocent were sailors. Not ones from Abra'am, interestingly. These sailors came from Eve, and they were eager to go home.

A LETTER WAS PENNED to a young Mesidian. It wouldn't reach her for some time, especially given the cold of winter and the turmoil occurring throughout the country, but when it did, it would hopefully grant her enormous relief.

I was innocent, and your father set me free, the letter said. *I was the last person to see him before he died. He loved you very much.*

Whatever you've been told of Dravian Valcor, know this: he lived and breathed and died for you. I will never be able to repay him.

I thought you should have this. It was his, and he gave it to me to help fend off the cold.

If the letter eventually reached the Mesidian, it would come alongside a box with a dark blue cloak inside.

Though she wasn't usually one to drink, X'odia enjoyed the rare sunlight shining down, accepted the cup Azgar handed her, and took a swig.

Much of Riverdee's suffering had ended. Not all, but much. With it, much of hers had too.

The city now knew her face, her name, her swirling eyes, and her wild hair.

That would've frightened her once.

It didn't frighten her anymore.

CHAPTER SIXTY
NATALIA

Becca, as Gwenivere, was put on trial.

She was outfitted in clothing that hid her curves. Her mother, ever the perfectionist, had put creams and powders on her face to make her cheeks look more hollowed and her brows more arched.

There was nothing to be done about her eyes. They were blue, thankfully, but not the turquoise color Natalia had always been jealous of.

It wouldn't matter. No one was going to get close enough to see them anyway.

Peter hosted a briefing to convey the news. He was still mad at Natalia, but he took his role seriously and made the announcement as his role required.

"Is it really her?" he'd asked in private. "Can I see her?"

"No."

Natalia hadn't clarified which question she'd been answering.

Though Gwenivere hadn't been seen by most people besides Garron, her father, and a handful of others around the palace, there were still a few knights with long careers who would've spotted the differences between her and Becca. The trial was closed, then, rather than being turned into a spectacle, with only the most thoroughly vetted writers present to serve as witnesses. No palace staff were allowed to enter, and only knights who'd never seen Gwenivere up close were allowed in, with the exceptions of Maximus and Nicolas, who were in on the plot.

As far as Abra'am knew, Gwenivere Verigrad was sentenced to a life of exile and imprisonment.

Given Aden had never believed his sister responsible for his father's death, it hadn't been difficult for Natalia and Vel to convince him of the plan.

"The imposter is willing, so long as she is compensated," Natalia had told him. "No harm will actually come to her, and we can call off the search on your sister."

Aden had agreed.

Vel had wanted to say goodbye to him. Though it was her own daughter's safety she cared about most of all, she still loved the boy. He was a sign of hope for Xenith, a pure soul who could be forged into a fine king, if the steel was shaped correctly.

She couldn't say goodbye, of course. If she did, she'd have to explain why she was leaving, and if that news got out, the chances of Anastasia finding out increased. Natalia and Vel might've been what the other feared, but that didn't mean the Prianthian woman wasn't still a threat. After months of looking over their shoulders, the Mistress of Birds and the Queen Regent understood it was best to operate with a suspicious eye.

"Take good care of our king," Vel had said, as she'd packed her things. "And take good care of this country."

That'd been it. Those had been the last words spoken between them.

Vel had traveled through the palace's secret halls, and when the trial was over, and the sentence was brought down, Natalia had Becca reunited with her mother.

Her sisters were there too. Vel had revealed the truth to them, about what she did and who she was, and she made it clear they had to leave the country.

It was surreal now, and oddly emotional, to watch the family of Verigrads prepare to flee. Maybe it was simply that Natalia was jealous. Maybe it was nice to do a good deed for someone else and give them a chance to start fresh, away from the machinations that'd held them captive for so long.

Becca and her family had decided to go to Riverdee. Natalia thought that a good choice. A small rebellion had just happened there, if she understood the rumors correctly, but the rebellion appeared to have made the country safer, rather than more dangerous.

"Goodbye, Lady Natalia," Becca said, bowing to her. "I hope the ambassador from Tiador enjoys the tea you make him."

"Goodbye to you too," Natalia said. She dipped her head, not enjoying the stirring in her chest, and gave a small wave. "I hope you enjoy the ocean."

She didn't watch them leave. There were too many other things to do, as was always the case. Walking back through the palace's hidden passageways, she headed up to her rooms and prepared her notes for the morning meeting.

It took her nearly half an hour to remember she wouldn't be having her morning meetings anymore. Realizing that, she poured herself a glass of wine, sat by the fire, and savored the quiet.

CHAPTER SIXTY-ONE
RYNARA

The first thing Rynara saw when she came to was a fist. It slammed into her face, nearly knocking her back into darkness. Whoever struck her lifted her up by her vest, pulled their fist back, and struck her again.

She gasped from the pain. Both hits landed on her temple. Her head throbbed, and her vision went black.

Orienting herself, Rynara placed her hands on the ground, attempting to sit up.

A foot kicked at her ribs.

"Enough."

As her eyes adjusted, Rynara rolled over, looking up.

She locked eyes with an older man. He looked Sadiyan, save his eyes, which were black in the dim light.

Not Sadiyan. Prianthian.

She thought he'd come to save her. Large men stood behind him, all forming a circle around her.

The small man stared at her with shrewd eyes, contemplative.

He was stooped, though not just from looking down. Wrinkles creased around his eyes. When he frowned, not much changed, save the cast of his mouth. The lines etched into his cheeks remained the same.

"Beat or break, but do not stab or sever," he ordered. He turned to one of the men beside him. "And that includes her ears."

Rynara was able to make out the man as the one whose ear she'd bitten off weeks before.

He glared at the restriction but nodded.

The old man backed up, and the others closed in. Rynara stumbled to her feet, but whatever had pulled her under before stole her balance. She swayed, trying to right herself, and prepared to *call* her elements.

They didn't answer. It was then she realized there were shackles on her wrists.

The big man lunged. Lethargic, Rynara barely managed to duck. His weight carried him far. He nearly fell into the others around him.

Another man came from her left, kicking the same side that'd been hit before. She grunted, falling, but hurriedly got back up, just as someone else grabbed her from behind.

They wrapped their arm around her throat and squeezed. She brought her chained hands up, instinct telling her *she needed to breathe, she needed to breathe, she needed to breathe.*

She forced her mind to calm, searching through foggy memories for a way out of the hold.

Seconds later, the maimed man came forward, remaining fist clenched.

He made to punch her stomach, but she leaned into the person behind her and lifted her legs. She caught the fist between them, squeezing, and if she could follow through—if she could *just* follow through—she'd be able to snap his arm.

The person behind her kept her pinned. All she could do was release the fist.

She had to get out of the hold. She'd pass out if she didn't.

Her hands were chained, but still free. She reached up from her captor's arms and toward their eyes. They screamed when she found them and began to press.

They let her go. She collapsed, gasping for breath.

The missing-eared man was there again. He struck her stomach, knocking the wind from her.

She vomited immediately. He shoved her, disgusted, but he'd shoved her back into the person who'd held her before. They kicked her knees out, sending her to the ground, then struck her face.

More kicks came. More fists. Rynara curled up in a ball, hands shielding her face, arms protecting her core.

It made little difference. The crows had come to feast, and she was their only meal.

She prayed for the beating to end and welcomed the blow that finally knocked her out.

Rynara's head throbbed.

Whatever had made her movements thick and syrupy

before was gone. Her head was clear, despite the pain, allowing her to look around.

She was in the Cave of Death and Dreams. She recognized the mushrooms and the crack letting in light above her. She winced when she looked up. The sun's rays went straight through her eyes and into her skull.

She'd never thought light could be so painful.

Coming further to, she tried remembering how she'd gotten to the place; not just the caves, but the Sanctuary itself. She remembered people saying the word as she'd been carried off. She remembered being paralyzed and wanting to scream, but her limbs wouldn't move, and her voice wouldn't come.

Garron. They'd taken Garron. She'd run back to her rooms. In case she was caught trying to find him, she'd not wanted her Amulet tied to her arm.

She'd untied it and strapped it to her ankle, beneath her pant legs and her boots. People would be so concerned about the *touched* knives strapped to her thighs than they wouldn't think to search her further, if they found those.

Fighting to move now, Rynara wriggled her ankle. The binding was still there. It was still tight. Her knives were gone, unsurprisingly, but as long as they hadn't found her Amulet, she'd hopefully be safe.

Maybe not safe, but safer than she would be otherwise. If the Redeemers found out they held a royal captive, they'd slaughter her.

Relieved, Rynara concentrated, trying to remember the rest.

She'd repositioned her Amulet. When she'd come out of her rooms, she'd meant to find Teniv and Dietrich. She'd hoped Dietrich and Seera would help her catch up to Garron quickly, while Teniv could let the other Hawks know the plan had gone awry.

Had she carried out those orders?

No. She'd been about to. When she'd stepped out of her rooms, someone had been waiting. They'd placed a cloth to her face.

She'd batted their hands away and struck them, but it hadn't mattered. Whatever had been on the cloth—a product of the mushrooms, likely—had made her lose consciousness. She'd been in and out after that until. . . .

The pain in her ribs reminded her.

She'd been beaten.

She didn't want to open her eyes again, but she forced herself to. The light still hurt, but she let her eyes adjust and glanced first at herself, then at her surroundings.

She was chained. The throbbing in her head was no doubt from the strikes she'd taken to the temple, but the elemental metal compounded it. Wearing the chains from time to time had been a part of Garron's training so that someday, when she was responsible for sentencing prisoners, she'd know what exactly she was sentencing them to.

He'd also wanted her to grow accustomed to the sensation, if ever she were to find herself in the position she was in now. People panicked when they were separated from their *auroras*. It caused them to make mistakes, and mistakes, while held captive, could lead to death.

Besides the chains, she noted that she was tied to a pole in the ground. It kept her sitting upright, and she had a horrible crick in her neck from it hanging to one side most of . . . the night? The day? She had no way of knowing.

Her clothes were the same ones she'd worn before. She smelled of vomit, sweat, and the dank wrongness of the caves.

Her ribs were maybe cracked. Her lip was split. Dried blood had crusted beneath her nose. When she lifted her brows, she could feel stinging above one of them. When she tilted her neck, something on her right side throbbed.

All in all, not horrible. Her wrists and arms and legs ached but didn't seem broken. If she attempted to stand—if the ropes weren't holding her down—she imagined she could do so relatively well. It would be a nightmare to try and fight again, and simple movements would no doubt be painful, but she could work with this. She just had to keep calm.

Her surroundings were underwhelming. Whatever parts of the caves she found herself in were not the parts where labor was conducted. She could hear it, though. The echo of warbled conversation carried to her, orders spoken loudly, and acknowledgments given timidly. Clanging told her they had a forge. To make weapons, likely to sell, and to man their followers.

A forge meant they had fire. Watching Dietrich work with poisons and cures told her fire was often needed when experimenting. Different temperatures created different results. Sometimes a gas had different properties than something as a liquid.

If she could just see around the cave wall and down the corridor dimly lit at the room's end, she might be able to get information. Garron was supposedly taken to the mines, but maybe after they'd captured her, they'd brought him back here.

She had no idea why they might do that, but logic, in this area at least, had left her.

She needed some seed of hope. She needed something to keep her going.

A door opened nearby. The old man she'd seen before came in. Rynara thought to close her eyes and feign sleep, but he'd seen her too quickly. She followed his movements as he walked toward her, surprised by his slow gait.

She'd been around the elderly before. Sir Charles had been ancient, but he'd not moved like this man. There was a difference between someone who walked with difficulty due to old injuries and one who walked with a back hunched from books, and shoulders bunched from never being told to stand straight.

He's not a warrior, she thought. *I don't think he even knows how to throw a punch.*

She knew looks could be deceiving, but unless this man was acting, she was certain he couldn't keep up in a fight.

"Phoenix," he said, taking off his spectacles and sliding them into his pocket. "We meet at last."

"May I speak?" she asked. Her throat was sore, and it hurt to talk, but she kept her voice distinguished. As much as she hated this man, she was a queen, regardless of whether he knew it or not. Today would not be the first time she sat across from an enemy. Her impulse to spit at him and tell him to burn for all eternity would do nothing to help her, her people, or her cause.

"Such deference," he said, smiling. He beckoned to someone, and Rynara watched as a young woman brought out a simple chair and set it down in front of Rynara. The woman retreated back down the corridor, and the old man sat. Even that movement seemed to strain him.

"Yes, you make speak," he said. Rynara recalled that before she'd been beaten, it was this man who'd told the others not to stab or sever. He might not be the one who delivered the blows, but he was the one who delivered orders.

Best not to anger him.

"If it suits you," she started, "you may call me Rynara. Or Ryn. What shall I call you?"

He smiled again, amused. "You may call me Navar."

This was Navar? This was the mastermind who'd destroyed

Deitrich's life, upended the harmony in the East, and unsettled the peace of Xenith and Riverdee?

She bit her tongue, but he must've read something on her face.

He laughed. "Surprised?"

She stared at him, trying to determine if he was lying. "Yes, actually."

"How did you imagine me?" His voice was pleasant. Soothing, almost. It made her uneasy.

"Frightening."

"What does frightening look like to you?"

My father, she thought. "I don't know."

"You're not quite what I imagined either," he admitted. "Your reputation seems larger than life. And the name: The Phoenix. It's so grand."

He sounded delighted, as if he was telling a bedtime story to his grandchild.

"Yet here you are," he continued. "Barely old enough to call yourself an adult. How old are you? Eighteen summers? Nineteen?"

"Twenty-two," she answered.

"Twenty-two." He shook his head, amazed. "I've not seen you fight properly, but most couldn't deflect a single blow with that much Cave Dust in their system. You have good instincts. I thought the stories exaggerated before, but now I think I must've been wrong."

Rynara didn't say anything. The man seemed to enjoy hearing himself talk, and if he did it enough, he might actually reveal something worthwhile.

Until then, it was best to keep her own talking to a minimum. Especially given how unnerving she found him.

"Do you know why I brought you here?"

Rynara shook her head.

"Do you want to take a guess?"

"Hostage?" she asked.

He smiled and pointed a finger at her. She thought he might bop her nose with it.

"Hostage."

"Do you want coin?"

"Oh, some, though I have plenty of that." He shifted in his seat, lacing his fingers over his stomach. He wasn't a large man in any capacity, but there was a softness around his core common in men of his age.

"Connections?" she offered, sensing he wanted her to keep guessing.

"Connections indeed. You seem to have a great deal of them."

"I don't really," she said honestly. "I have wealthy friends. That's about the extent of it."

"You've removed so many of my followers, though."

She shrugged. "The West covets its wealth. You've disrupted that, and now you're seeing the result."

"Is that what you are? Wealthy?"

"No. I'm like you in some ways. I saw something I thought should change, and I tried to be the catalyst for it."

"I see."

He pulled a river stick from his pocket, lighting the end with a small fire element. He tapped the rest back into his coat. It wasn't particularly cold in the caves, but with his age, she imagined he felt the cold more acutely. The rest of his clothes, brown, and simple, like a priest or a librarian, looked to be lined with some kind of fur.

"Would you like one?" he asked, noting her stare.

She shook her head. "I don't smoke those."

"Would you like to try?" he whispered conspiratorially.

"I'm afraid it might hurt a bit." She tapped her split lip. "Thank you, though."

"I must say, you are far more dignified than I expected. Most rebel leaders are brash and outspoken."

She snorted. "I've been called those things and more plenty of times."

"What is it about me you feel doesn't warrant such traits?"

"These, in part," she said, holding up her chained wrists. "I remember the beating quite well too."

"Fear of pain, then?"

"No. Logic. I know pain well. I'm just not stupid enough to antagonize someone into making me feel more of it."

"Tell me, child, what is it you want?"

She was taken aback by the question.

"What do I want?"

"Yes. You said you wanted change. What does change look like to you?"

"It..."

She'd been about to answer, but stopped. A serviceable answer would not suffice. Navar hadn't accomplished all he had over the last thirty years because he'd approached what he'd wanted with simplicity. He seemed a man of conviction, one who'd surveyed different paths, ruled out those that wouldn't best serve him, and cautiously traversed those that might. To answer quickly would be to lose his respect. He'd granted her some of that, to start. If she gave the wrong answer, or a hasty one, that respect would slip away.

"I see much wrong in Xenith's makeup," she answered truthfully. "Since I was a child, I thought my country was blessed. I was taught that and told that over and over. People said we had much, because we were great, and scholarly.

"I used to look at the palace of Voradeen and wonder why one family needed so much, when others had so little—and so little was only considering other Xens. Many people in other countries have far less than the lowest in mine.

"I learned, though, that Xenith is not blessed. It has much because it has taken much. I do not agree with how you implement your ideas, but I agree that the West is corrupt."

"You explained *what* you want to change," he said, blowing out a small plume of smoke. "You haven't explained what that change looks like."

"Our views," she said. "How Xens see themselves. I want my people to look at what they have, and instead of asking how they could have more, I want them to see what they have and be grateful, then look at what they can give. I want them to not care if someone's eyes are green, or blue, or gold. I want us to not see ourselves as set apart and better, simply because of where we were born and the arbitrary lines on a map."

"Funny," he replied, though his tone belied the word. "So much of what you seem to hate is from your own people. Why, then, do you go after mine?"

"You feed the pigs," she said. "You're taking advantage of those who want wealth. You've made your fortune from them and expanded your reach, all while they fill their pockets and look the other way. If I take out that which feeds them, I can take them out too."

"I see. And once my influence has been removed, what will you do?"

Rynara didn't like the quality his voice had taken. It reminded her of when she'd thrown a tantrum as a child, knowing she was wrong to do so, but having an adult force her to explain her reasoning for their own amusement, rather than explaining why her reasoning was wrong.

"Build an army," she answered truthfully. "I want to rule, and rule justly."

"What lofty goals you have."

She ground her teeth.

Yes, he was most certainly patronizing her.

"Do you know where the problem lies in this?" he asked.

She shook her head.

"You think to build atop a broken foundation. I agree with you; the West is corrupt. Xenith most of all. But you wish to patch that which festers. An infection will spread throughout the body from the hand, yet you only wish to trim the fingernails. I have lived much longer than you. I know what the world is missing, and what it's missing is *balance*."

He said the word like it was a grand truth. A profound secret.

"Imagine I hold up two scales." He lifted his hands, one high, one low. "This here is the West, as it stands now, and this here is the East. The West has built itself up, more and more and more, and the East has plummeted. In recent years, the West has insisted it will work with Sadie, and it will help it become an established, steady nation. And while yes, some of their trade has helped Sadie prosper, it is *you* who prospers the most."

He raised his lowered hand minimally, and his lifted hand greatly.

"Let us now imagine that we wipe everything clean."

He lowered both hands.

"The West builds itself up on its own, and Sadie, Prianthia, and perhaps Yendor, build themselves up on their own. That would be fair. That would be justice."

"Turning people into slaves is justice?" she asked, glaring. "Killing innocent people is justice?"

He laughed.

The sound filled her gut with fire.

"I didn't claim everyone must die," he said, taking another

drag from the stick. "I merely believe the scales should return to level."

"If not death, and slavery, then what? What does this change look like to you?"

His amusement faded. He studied her through the small bit of smoke drifting around his face.

Respect. He respected her. He liked that she'd thrown his question back to him.

Rynara felt disgusted. Even if it kept her safe, she found she didn't want this man's respect.

"Some will die," he admitted. "Many, truth be told. Many more will lose their homes, and their wealth. They'll have to toil the fields, and work for themselves, rather than build their empire off of someone else's back."

"The trade ban," she said, eyeing him. "You want the trade ban in place, don't you?"

"Of course! The trade ban is the best thing to happen between the West and East in decades. It's forced each country to think for itself. I control the cures now, and I determine who gets to live and who gets to die. Is that not what you want too? To play the role of nature? You said yourself that you don't like the pigs I feed. You wish to feed those *you* deem worthy. I am the same. We just have different definitions of who deserves to be fed."

"No." Her fingernails dug into her palms. "I don't want to determine who is fed. I want people to know contentment. Those are two very different things. You feed the worst among us. You use the corrupt for your own gain. If you cared about balancing the scales, you wouldn't reward those who only see people as tools."

"I do what is necessary," he countered. "I will concede the point that many I work with are fiend-infested filth. They care little for anyone. They're despicable."

He tossed what was left of his stick to the floor and crumpled it under his boot.

"But I am a man who knows change does not happen quickly. I will die someday soon. I need to ensure that systems are in place to keep the gears going. You are young and idealistic. You will learn in time what it takes to enact change."

Before he could say more, the woman who'd brought his chair returned. She seemed timid as she approached. She had a set of printings in her hand.

Navar smiled pleasantly and beckoned her over, as one might call a child who'd picked out a book to be read. The woman hurried over, eyes flicking down to Rynara for a moment before facing Navar.

She handed him the parchments. He made to put his spectacles back on, then grew frustrated when he still couldn't determine what the printing said.

"Just tell me," he said, waving his hand.

"In front of . . ."

The woman looked again to Rynara.

"Who's she going to tell?" he asked, laughing.

The woman licked her lips.

"We've lost Riverdee. X'odia Daer'dee escaped and raided all of our storerooms. She's handed out cures and coins to the people and turned over seventy of our followers there."

Rynara's eyes widened. It hurt to do so, but it was worth it to get a full view of Navar's shock.

Whoever this X'odia woman was, she and Teniv had been wrong to underestimate her. Navar too, if she had to guess.

You will see that it's not you that the Light blesses, but me, she remembered the printing saying.

If she ever escaped this place, she'd have to find a way to meet this woman.

"Also," the reader went on. "News from the capital has said

that Gwenivere Verigrad has been captured, put on trial, exiled, and imprisoned. The throne is saying the princess was turned over by Sadiyans as an act of good faith. It's being predicted that the Treaty of Five, upon meeting with an ambassador from Tiador, will vote to lift the ban."

That news made little sense, but it didn't matter. Rynara smiled openly as Navar stood and fumed. The man looked like he might heave his chair or strike the woman, but he settled for pacing and throwing up his hands.

"Tell Anastasia!" he ordered, struggling to calm himself. "She'll need to give Victor new commands."

"Yes, sir."

He looked to Rynara. She made no effort to hide her grin.

"Have this one whipped. I need her followers."

The woman hesitated.

"Y-Yes, sir."

CHAPTER SIXTY-TWO
DIETRICH

Dietrich had never known three days could last so long.

Teniv had justifiably suspected him when Gwenivere was taken. After word from the Hawks traveled her way, it'd been discovered that their ins with Sarabai's enforcers had been found out. Information had been beaten out of them, including the locations of Teniv's warehouse, where she and Gwenivere had been staying and what they knew about the Sanctuary.

Fortunately, Gwenivere and Teniv had ensured that no single person knew the names of every Hawk. They all were parts of a web.

Teniv and Garron had told Gwenivere that it was better that they knew more than her, in case she was ever taken captive. That way, if they were to beat information out of her, she wouldn't reveal each remaining piece of the web.

Dietrich prayed now that Gwenivere's stubbornness wouldn't push through. He hoped she'd offer up whatever information they asked of her.

He revealed quickly to Teniv that he knew who Gwenivere really was. The faster him and the woman could swap what knowledge they had of the other, the better. If Gwenivere's identity was found out, the Redeemers wouldn't just make an example of her to the Hawks. They'd parade her head around all of Sarabai and spread word of her capture around the city.

The first day was awful, but some good news had come. Apparently, a false Gwenivere had been captured in the capital. None of the Hawks could see Teniv and Dietrich react to that news, but privately, the two had collectively breathed a sigh of relief.

"Must be a way to pull attention from some other crisis," Teniv said. "Makes me feel sorry for the poor girl they convicted, but I'll take it, if it means keeping the suspicion off Gwenivere."

For the sake of transparency, Dietrich told Teniv, as briefly and succinctly as possible, who he was and everything he had and hadn't done in recent months.

"No, I didn't kill the Laighless family."

"No, I didn't kill Prince Roland."

"No, I don't know who did it."

"I don't know where he is."

"My brother and I hatched the assassination attempt in Sovereignty together."

"Yes, I'm still fighting against the Redeemers."

"Yes, I have a dragon."

It'd taken far more hours than he would've liked to prove himself to the former soldier, though in some ways, he was grateful for her skepticism. As long as the Redeemers held Gwenivere, there really wasn't much they could do. They might be able to craft some plan to get her out, but until the three-day mark came, he doubted they could do much without either putting her in harm's way or getting themselves captured alongside her.

"Trust me, boy," Teniv had told him. "Leaders are taken all the time. Usually, the other side wants something. As long as we have something Navar wants, he's not going to kill her."

"He might hurt her, though."

Teniv's face looked calm, but her neck muscles tensed.

"That he might."

Seera?

Dietrich stood at his desk, staring at his vials. If he'd been able to figure something out, none of this would've happened. They'd have liberated the Sanctuary, kept Garron from being sent to the mines, and kept Gwenivere from being used as a hostage.

Are you sure you want to know?

Dietrich locked his jaw.

Yes.

They've hurt her. She was whipped and beaten. They've not done anything else.

Dietrich put a fist to his mouth.

He would kill them.

I should come out there. I should—

No. The breaking *may work both ways. If you go into a frenzy, you may send me into one too. We can't risk that.*

Fine.

He fought the urge to punch a wall.

And Garron?

I'm sorry. I lost track of him in the mountains. He was alive, last I saw, but I believe they are truly sending him to the mines.

Dietrich couldn't even give Gwenivere that. It would be the hope she would cling to when he'd see her again in three days. He didn't want to lie to her, but he also didn't want to tell her the truth.

He's my favorite person in the world, she'd said.

He reached out to his dragon again. *What do I do, Seera?*

She was silent. Even with the distance between them, he could feel her shifting.

Rest, as much as you can, she finally answered. *And be ready. She will need that from you.*

Dietrich wiped at his brow, took a breath, and tried to do as his dragon suggested.

They had to meet at the cave's entrance. Seera had never seen anyone go through the front when they'd first taken Gwenivere, which meant there were other ways into the cave. Likely not wanting any Hawks to spot them, the Redeemers had sent orders along that they would meet a maximum of four people at the cave's front.

Teniv was too valuable to go. All the Hawks agreed that the woman had to stay back in case the meeting was a trap. She'd suggested Dietrich go, introducing him as Yeltaire Veen, the new recruit who'd found the tradesmen and gotten the Sanctuary's location in the first place. Dietrich, along with a Prianthian man named Gregor—who they thought might be helpful in case anything needed translating—a Sadiyan woman named Sasha, and a Xen woman named Antigone were the four chosen. They all covered their faces as they approached the caves.

Dietrich hardly recognized Gwenivere when they brought her out.

Her face was swollen. Bruises lined her cheeks, and an ink mark had been etched into the side of her neck. Dried blood stuck in her hair.

The two men on either side of her held her arms as though she might try to flee. Chains clinked between her wrists. When she was brought out into the light, just outside the cave, she winced.

"Turn her around," a man ordered.

Along with the two Redeemers at her sides, another person accompanied them. He was an older man, Prianthian, and dressed in simple garb. The Redeemers obeyed him, turning Gwenivere so her back was exposed.

Antigone cried out. Sasha cursed, and Gregor, big as he was, let out a quiet gasp.

Calm yourself, Seera ordered. Dietrich had instinctively reached for his knives.

Gwenivere's back was covered in ugly slashes. Dietrich had never seen such wounds fresh, but he knew what the scars would look like.

Culter had them. His father's back had been covered in them.

Most every person in Sadie over their fourth decade had them.

Gwenivere hadn't just been beaten.

She'd been whipped.

I want to kill them, Dietrich thought, grinding his teeth.

Seera, as best she could, sent back a wave of calm.

There will be time yet for them to die.

"Turn her back," the old man ordered. The Redeemers once again did as commanded, spinning Gwenivere back around. Dietrich could see now that, though she had little control over where her arms lay, she was purposefully trying to hold them up to cover her chest. There was nothing holding her breasts in place.

Do not feel shame, he wanted to tell her. *Your Hawks could see you stripped naked, and you would still be their Phoenix.*

He couldn't say that though. None of them could. They could only meet her eyes and pretend they didn't want to cry for all the suffering she'd endured.

I know her reservations, he thought. It'd taken nearly a month for her to even allow herself to be held. She'd allowed more after that to Dietrich, far more than he'd ever expected, but he knew it was rare for her.

To be stripped of such modesty was no shame, but guarded as she was, she would feel it as such.

"Where is Teniv?" the old man asked. "I wish to meet her."

Gwenivere had given up names, then. Good. They'd trained her to do so. It would keep her alive.

"In the city," Dietrich answered. It'd been agreed upon before that he would speak. "She didn't know her presence was requested."

"She is a woman of much wealth," Navar said. "And much influence. I'll give you back your Phoenix, if Teniv gives us all of her investments, coin, the taverns she owns, and information on all of her contacts."

Almost imperceptibly, Gwenivere shook her head.

"We want her," Dietrich said, nodding Gwenivere's way, "and all the others you hold captive in the Sanctuary."

The old man laughed.

"No. You forget, boy, I am not Sadiyan. I do not haggle. I set out my wares, and if you want them, you will have them. You need only pay the price."

Wares. That's what Gwenivere was to him. A thing to be bought and sold.

"Write down everything from Teniv you wish to have," Dietrich said. "We will relay your offer back to her."

It killed something in him to say it, but it was only a stalling tactic. As Teniv had said, so long as the Hawks had something the Redeemers wanted, they'd keep Gwenivere alive. Dietrich just couldn't imagine her enduring more than she already had. He didn't want to walk away without her.

"How about this," the old man said, stroking the stubble along his chin. "I will write down all of what I know Teniv to have, and you will write down all of what Teniv has. That way, I know that you aren't selling me short."

"I don't know what she has."

"Find out then."

Dietrich clenched his fists.

"How long before I have to send this message?"

The old man hummed, thinking.

"Three more days."

Three more days. Dietrich didn't think he could do it. It'd been difficult enough to know Gwenivere had been at their mercy. Seeing now what they'd done to her, and imagining what more they might do, made his hands shake.

"No new wounds," he said, gesturing to Gwenivere. "If you promise she won't incur any new wounds, then I'll return in three days with the list."

"Deal."

"We wish to speak with her."

The old man had looked ready to depart back into the cave. He glanced at Dietrich, then at the other three Hawks, then to his own men.

"Go on, then," he said. "Talk."

Dietrich didn't want to speak in front of everyone, but he wasn't foolish enough to think he'd be given a moment alone with her.

"Are . . ." He licked his lips, trying to think how best to word his question.

"The stars," he finally said. He hoped she'd understand his meaning. "If you feel like you're losing hope, look to the stars."

The original plan. That's what he was referencing. If Garron had gone into the Sanctuary, the goal was to send him notes through the cracks in the cave's ceiling.

That was still their plan. They'd have to be careful, but if he could get notes to her, maybe there'd be a chance of finally determining how to liberate the Sanctuary, and Gwenivere with it.

She narrowed her eyes, then slowly nodded.

"I will," she said. "I will look to the stars always, whether I lose hope or not. I will know that my Hawks look upon them too, and I will feel renewed."

The old man seemed to have had enough. He spun his hand in a circle, signaling his followers back into the cave.

"Three days!" he called, waving. "I'll see you in three days."

With that, Gwenivere was gone.

CHAPTER SIXTY-THREE
RYNARA

Navar kept his promise. He didn't have any new wounds inflicted.

That didn't mean he hadn't found ways to still cause her pain.

Though the heat was bearable, sunlight burned, regardless of temperature. Navar ordered her tied in the same cave she'd been in before, though this time, it was by her neck, rather than her torso, so that her back faced the sunlight coming through the cracks.

All day she sat, body bruised and aching. The open slits across her back stung. It almost seemed worse than when she'd been whipped. That had been excruciating, but the strikes themselves had been over in minutes. This, this all-day stiffness, the inability to move and protect her wounds, was agonizing. She nearly cried from relief when the sun shifted, and her back was no longer burning. She had maybe twenty minutes before someone noticed, and repositioned her.

Those twenty minutes were her greatest reprieve.

"You're the Phoenix," Navar said mockingly. "Where else are your wings to sprout from, if not your back?"

In the evening she was untied and brought to a new part of the Sanctuary. She stumbled several times, then gasped at the pain. There wasn't any specific wound she winced from. All of them screamed for her to rest.

She thought she might pass out. Her back felt hot and stung and itched, while the rest of her felt cold. Sweat dripped from her brow and down her neck. She shook, though there was plenty of warmth from the Sanctuary's fires.

She'd been right about the forge. Redeemers were making weapons. Forcing her eyes to take in everything she could, she noted the impossibly massive cavern beneath her, where rows upon rows of slaves sat. Like her, they all had chains around their wrists, though they could get up and move relatively freely. Redeemers stood guard around tunnel entrances. No one seemed hurt, thankfully, but still, the cave was a prison, and whatever they worked to make was poisoning her country.

"Come now," her captor told her, noticing her stares. "I need to get you patched up."

The person walking with her was the same one who'd nervously delivered information to Navar. She seemed far more at ease, now, confident, even, as she led Rynara across stone walkways. There were no natural railings through the caves, but the Redeemers must've created some, as metal bars ran along the edges where she and the woman walked. Several times, Rynara slipped on the slick moss beneath her and caught a railing to steady herself. Cursing, she felt liquid drip down her back. She tried not to wonder what it was.

The woman eventually led her to a small room with a cot. Rynara hoped she'd not be forced to sleep there. Dietrich's words, if she'd deciphered them correctly, were to inform her that he'd try and message her throughout the night. This room, simple as it was, only held the makeshift bed, a chair, and a dresser. The woman guided Rynara to the bed, helping to ease her onto her stomach, then slipped on a pair of gloves and pulled jars from the dresser's drawers.

Wordlessly, she opened one of the jars, pulled a glob of white salve from it, and began rubbing it on Rynara's back. She hissed, both from the pain and the coolness, but the woman shushed her gently, and pushed her down.

"It stings at first," she said, "but it will help."

A *healer*, Rynara thought. She clasped tightly to the sheet on the cot, grinding her teeth as the woman continued her ministrations.

When she'd finished, she pulled Rynara upright and checked her other wounds. None were as horrible as those on her back, thankfully, but even if she understood that logically, it didn't make her feel any better. She still could hardly think, given how horribly she'd been injured and burned.

Bandaging came next. It hurt everywhere, but especially on the lashings, and when the woman tightened them, the pressure on her ribs made her groan.

"Am I to endure this again tomorrow?" she asked weakly.

"I will advise Navar to give you a day of rest."

She attempted a nod.

"Thank you."

"My name is Nayva, by the way."

Rynara tried to have the will to care. "Why do you do this?"

It's not what she'd meant to say, but it's what came out. The woman, Nayva, lifted a brow.

"Do what? Heal?"

"Work for them. There are no chains on your wrists. You're here willingly, I assume?"

Nayva turned away, sliding the jar lid back on and returning it to the dresser.

"Look."

She grabbed at either end of her robes, and pulled down, exposing her chest. Instinctively, Rynara made to turn away but stopped when she saw the woman's scars.

She had no breasts. In their place only lay a crisscrossing of lines.

She pulled her robes back up.

"I'm Sadiyan, as I'm sure you can tell." She gestured to her dark hair and green eyes. "I married a Prianthian man. Can you guess who did this to me?"

Rynara shook her head. "Any group is capable of evil, I've found."

Nayva let out a small snort. "Yes, well, my own family did this to me. They said that this way, I'd never be able to feed the fiend that came out of my womb. Then they killed my husband. The Redeemers took me in; they were the *only* ones who'd take me in. Too many of my brethren told me I deserved this."

She pulled something else from a drawer, then lifted a pitcher of water Rynara hadn't noticed, and poured her a drink.

"Take these," she said. "You have a fever. These will help."

Rynara did as she was told. The small tablets Nayva handed her were bitter, but she gulped them down quickly with the water, and handed back the glass.

"I'm sorry," Rynara said. "For what was done to you. I can't imagine that level of condemnation, especially from my own family."

"You would feel sympathy for me, when I was the one who brought you here?"

Rynara narrowed her eyes. She didn't remember clearly who'd put the cloth to her mouth at the inn, but Nayva had all but confessed, and she had no reason to disbelieve her.

"How did you find me?"

"I got a job at the inn. I worked the front desk. It wasn't hard to figure out which room was yours after that."

Rynara nodded. She was too tired and in too much pain to do much else. Even expending anger toward this woman seemed exhausting.

"Even then," she muttered.

"What?"

"Even then. Knowing it was you. I still feel sympathy for you."

"I don't need your sympathy."

"No. You just need Navar's."

Nayva stared at her. Rynara hadn't meant it to sound so biting, but even said quietly, it seemed to awaken something in her.

Unspeaking, Nayva helped her up, bringing her back to the other cave room. Rynara took one more glance at the makeshift factory beneath them—makeshift town, truthfully, given its size—wishing she could see where all the tunnels led.

She also made every effort she could not to trip or stumble, lest she bring herself more pain.

When they reached the room, Rynara fought the impulse to look at the cracks in the ceiling. They weren't big enough for a person to fit through, but she wished somehow they were, and that Dietrich could come down, and grant her comfort.

She'd hated being presented to him and her Hawks, weak and harmed as she was. Not because she cared about herself, in that moment, but because she'd seen the anguish in them, the helplessness. If their roles were reversed, she knew she'd feel the same.

Be at peace, she thought. *I'll make it out of this.*

More than making it out for their sake, she had to make it out for her own. She needed to recover, gain back her strength, and find out where Garron had been taken. She refused to believe her knight had undergone any of the same misery she had. He was safe, somewhere, keeping his head down, minding his captors. He was being taken to a mine, likely, but he was strong, and they wouldn't want to hurt him for fear he'd make a less productive worker.

It wasn't a good fate, but it was one she could save him from.

Yes. She'd get out of this place. She'd find him.

"I'll be back," Nayva said. She deposited Rynara as if she was an unwieldy sack, then left. When she returned, she had a pillow and blanket. They'd do little to make the cave floor bearable, but with her newly bandaged back, she'd at least be able to cover it with the blanket. It was better than laying with her skin exposed. She didn't know what kinds of things the mushroom's pollutants did to open wounds.

Before leaving, Nayva also started a fire for her. It was small, and would probably burn out well before the night was through, but it confirmed to Rynara that fires could be started openly in this place. She hadn't been sure before. It seemed the workers had separate areas sectioned off for their labor to take place. At least now the mystery of whether open flames would react with the strange air had been solved.

"Thank you," Rynara said as Nayva made to leave.

The woman didn't answer her. She pulled the blanket over her back, then left, closing the door to the cave room behind her.

Rynara had no way of knowing if Dietrich was there. She might not have even understood his message correctly. Fatigue clung to her, a combination of too much pain, too little sleep, her fever, and whatever Nayva had given her.

She lay still on her stomach. The agony clinging to her wasn't gone, but it was manageable, if she didn't move. Looking for the little bit of brightness in all the darkness, she thanked the Light that Garron had forced her to work with element shackles, for she couldn't imagine how disoriented she'd feel if that had compounded atop everything else.

To comfort herself, she flexed her leg. She could feel the tie around her ankle, securing her Amulet.

She stared at the flames, wishing she could *call* to them. The chains were the least of her worries, but she might be able to free herself of this place, if only she could *call* her elements. It was odd to think she missed them. She'd not thought the feeling possible for something that didn't live, but she did miss them. She missed the power they gave her, and the freedom. She missed the security of knowing that no matter what, when she *called* to them, they answered.

She wished she could undo the effects of her chains.

A thought came to her, of what the Artifacts were meant to dp. A thought that had come to her often, when she'd wished to change her fate.

Ancient scripts hadn't been detailed, and the text being written in Old Evean made translations unreliable, but the traits of each Artifact were generally agreed upon by scholars.

The Dagger granted immortality, and the Shield granted invincibility.

The Ring could bind, and the Amulet could undo that which had been done.

Rynara took a breath, and attempted to do what she'd vowed never to do as a Guardian: she looked to the fire at her side and, willing it to obey her, *called* on her Artifact's power.

And the power answered.

CHAPTER SIXTY-FOUR
X'ODIA

For the first time in months, X'odia allowed herself to fall into a true restful slumber.

When she woke up, as she thought might occur, the Sight claimed her.

The vision was short.

It showed her a dragon, a man, and a woman on fire.

No, not on fire. The woman *was* the fire.

And she burned everything in sight.

CHAPTER SIXTY-FIVE
GWENIVERE

Gwenivere Verigrad stood. The wounds on her back sealed. The bruises faded.

She could *call* elements.

More than *call*.

Absorb.

The fire Nayva had made—the fire that was now *inside* her—had proven that.

She had to escape. She had to escape *tonight*. If the Redeemers discovered what she'd done, they'd kill her, or worse. They might take her Artifact. She had no idea the influence Navar would wield if he possessed that.

Dietrich's note finally came. It fluttered down to her from the crack above. With her pain gone, she was able to run over to it before it drifted further away.

With it came a bit of charcoal, so she could write back.

Are you all right? his note read.

Hurriedly, she wrote out her answer.

I'm fine. Is Seera with you?

She looked up, and cast the note to the small shadow

coming through the moonlight. She couldn't see Dietrich clearly, but she imagined he'd be surprised, when the parchment came back to him without his elements to bring it up.

She's here. Did they remove your chains?

No. But I don't have time to explain. I need you to trust me. Have Seera break through the ceiling until she can fill this cave with fire. Have her direct every flame aurora *she can at me. At me! I know it sounds absurd, but please, trust me.*

She sent the note back up.

Waited.

Outside, she could here Redeemers talking. If they came in and found her standing, they'd know something was amiss.

Come on come on come on!

She was practically jumping waiting for Dietrich's response.

He didn't send another note. She waited minutes, and those minutes felt like hours, given all that was at stake. She bounced on her heels, praying he'd hurry, praying he'd not overthink her command.

Trust me, she urged, willing her thoughts to him. *Trust—*

The room shook. A loud banging sounded against the ceiling. Gwenivere laughed, her blood stirring.

Come on, Seera, she thought. *Break this place to pieces.*

Outside her room, the Redeemers started shouting. The banging echoed throughout the caves, but its origin was indecipherable to any besides her.

They likely thought an earthquake was happening. They certainly wouldn't think to check the room with the half-dead hostage.

Seera's claw broke through. Gwenivere looked to it, excited, then back to the door. The claw lifted, disappearing, then burst through again. Rocks fell from the ceiling. Moonlight came in. When Seera pressed her claw through a third time, huge chunks of the ceiling fell. Gwenivere jumped out of the way, lest she be crushed.

It was then that door to her room finally opened. The men who'd taken turns beating her entered.

Gwenivere smiled.

"Now!"

As she'd commanded, Seera roared, and released an eruption of fire. Gwenivere *called* on her Artifact again, shouting as the fires engulfed her.

They didn't burn. Not her at least. The men who'd come into the room were reduced to ash, but Gwenivere's body remained upright. Like Seera's scales, and the chains on her wrists, her skin took the fire in. Her body filled with it.

Seera kept *calling* fire. Gwenivere absorbed it all, until she glowed with the red of embers and the orange of heat. There was no limit to what she could take. She was infinite flames.

She was power incarnate.

When Seera had nothing left, she continued to bang at the ground beneath her, ripping open the cave wall. Once the opening had grown big enough, she crashed down like a torrent, Dietrich atop her back.

"Gwenivere?"

She smiled up at him, then lifted her chains to the dragon.

Seera put her teeth around them, sunk in, and whipped her head back.

The chains snapped.

CHAPTER SIXTY-SIX
DIETRICH

G wenivere was a goddess. She was a star crashed down from the heavens. A meteor without flight.

Dietrich had never seen anything like it. The flames Seera *called* wrapped around and into Gwenivere's flesh. She stood beneath him, her skin aglow with fire.

He could feel the heat burning off her. It licked her skin, yet settled, as though she was the pull of gravity itself.

"The Redeemers are without chains," she said. "The slaves are in the cavern below."

Then she was off. Dietrich held tight to Seera's quills as Gwenivere ran through the open door at the room's edge. It was too small for Seera to fit through, but she'd broken down one cave wall already. What was a few more?

Ready, Prince? she asked, sensing his thoughts.

He crouched down low, and dropped his shoulders.

Seera roared, opened her wings, and barreled forward.

CHAPTER SIXTY-SEVEN
GWENIVERE

J ust as Gwenivere crossed the platform, Seera came bursting through.

All along the various walkways, Redeemers shouted, frantically trying to ready weapons. Those who *called* elements had them absorbed into Seera's scales. Those with *touched* bows tried to aim, only to have a column of fire erupt from Gwenivere's hands.

They screamed.

Their arms burned off.

Seera and Dietrich landed in the cavern below. Gwenivere lost sight of them as she liquefied Nayva's door and sprinted into her room.

"Leave now, if you want to live," Gwenivere ordered. The woman scurried to the room's back, but Gwenivere didn't waste time seeing if she listened. She ran back out, *called* air, and jumped to the cavern below.

Unlike the clock tower, there was no preparation. Gwenivere came down like a comet. Her ankles shattered from the impact.

Crying out, she *called* upon her Amulet, her bones reknitting themselves. Beneath her, the ground began to melt.

Dietrich leaped from Seera's back. He landed beside her, daggers ready. As Redeemers dropped their weapons and made to flee, they were struck down by Seera's claws, Gwenivere's flames, and Dietrich's blades.

"Kill them!"

Gwenivere looked up, expecting to find Navar's orders directed at her or Dietrich. Instead, the man was pointing to the hundreds of enslaved people huddled together.

"No!"

Gwenivere cast her fire out, but there were too many of them. Redeemers emerged from various tunnels throughout the cave, swarming the walkways above and casting elements down.

Navar would rather kill the enslaved then let them go. Gwenivere screamed, but there was nothing she could do.

They were going to die.

A gush of wind knocked her back. Seera hurled herself forward, her wings opening.

The enslaved wept and cried out, but the elements absorbed into Seera's scales.

Then she roared and flew toward the pathways above.

"Get them out!" Gwenivere yelled to Dietrich. He finished stabbing a Redeemer through the chest, kicking the man off his blade. He nodded to her and hurried over to the prisoners.

Gwenivere cast her fire toward the flurry of Redeemers readying arrows. They were like a swarm, a murder of crows emerging from the remnants of a hollowed-out tree. She pressed her flames toward them as Seera latched her claws onto one of the walkway's railings, grabbed three men in her jaws, and snapped them in half.

Their bodies landed with a smack at Gwenivere's side.

More men fell. Seera dug her claws through men's chests, then flicked them down. What'd been the slave quarters transformed into the Redeemers' deathplace. The cave would soon echo with the sound of their *auroras drifting*.

As Seera leaped from pathway to pathway, Gwenivere watched Navar disappear down a corridor. Trusting the dragon to defend herself and Dietrich to lead the enslaved people to safety, Gwenivere dashed through a cave hall.

She couldn't let Navar escape.

The light of her flaming body illuminated the dark labyrinth. She stopped to listen at a forked path, piercing through the screams and shouts of panic, listening for Navar's voice. When she'd found it, she made her way through the furthest corridor, praying to stop his flight.

Eleven men were running the opposite direction. Toward her, rather than away.

Four raised their spears. Two lifted crossbows. Five lifted swords.

Gwenivere caught her breath, sighed, and rushed them.

They'd not expected her advance. They struck out, some landing hits, slicing open her skin. A bolt shot through her shoulder. A spear slammed through her chest.

The weapons burned away instantly, saving her the trouble of pulling them out. Continuing to *call* on the Amulet, the wounds closed.

The men backed up, terrified. One dropped his crossbow as she approached. When she lifted her fist, he tried to shield his face, but the heat from her body melted through his arms. As her blow struck, the entire left side of his face burned off.

She struck out at the others around her. By the time she was through, she'd incurred slashes and stab wound, though none remained. The Redeemers were scattered around her, molten lava along the labyrinth floor.

Livid at the time they'd wasted, she stepped over what remained of them, and continued her pursuit.

CHAPTER SIXTY-EIGHT
DIETRICH

Dietrich led the prisoners. He'd not realized how far the Serpent's Breath had descended within the Sanctuary. It was a massive, waterless well plummeting down, down, down. His lungs burned from the uphill climb, the fight, and defending the enslaved as Redeemers pursued them.

His enemies should've run. They should've seen his size, his speed, his ease of movement, and retreated.

Instead, they tried to fight.

Where the Redeemers pursued, Dietrich left piles of bodies.

The captives who'd been brought in most recently and remembered the path told Dietrich which way to go. They'd determined swiftly that they were being freed. They were allies now. It'd not been a thing forged or a treaty signed. It was a chance of escape, and they'd clasped it strongly.

Many of the enslaved were children and elderly women. When it seemed no more Redeemers came, Dietrich sheathed his knives and lifted those who fell behind. He scooped two small boys up. A little girl, no older than her sixth winter, wrapped her legs around his stomach and her arms around his neck.

The strongest of them fell back, helping those who couldn't run as fast. The cracks on the ceiling were closed the further they went, leaving the caves in total darkness. Dietrich understood now why folktales told of an ancient, massive serpent slithering its way through the mountains. The tunnels were stories high and rounded out, smooth and slick above and beneath him.

With no moonlight to guide their feet, more and more people began to fall. Their feet now splashed through water, fatigued and tired. Dietrich urged them on, always looking over his shoulder, always afraid Navar's Redeemers would catch up and cut some of them down.

"Go!" he yelled. "Get up! We're almost there!"

He had no idea how much farther, but a few women in the front echoed the call.

There were some men among them. As Dietrich's steps began to slow, they ran over to him, giving him the same encouragement he'd given them. They each took one of the children he carried, leaving his body free to care only for itself.

"It's here!" someone shouted. "We've made it!"

A small circle of light formed at the tunnel's end. It sat above a pile of enormous rocks, remnants, it seemed, from a cave in long ago.

The sight of it, and the declaration, sent a wave of hope through them. Their pace quickened. Their energy reignited.

They'd done it. They'd liberated the Sanctuary.

All that was left was the small climb and they'd be among the forest.

Seera! Dietrich called. *Seera, where are you?*

In response, the dragon's claw once again burst through the cave wall. This time, it'd come from opposite of him. She'd already flown out of the cave and circled back around to this exit, sensing where he'd been within the mountain.

She pulled her claw back, widening the small escape. Moonlight shone down and illuminated the way to freedom.

Atop her back, still wreathed in flames, sat Gwenivere.

CHAPTER SIXTY-NINE
GWENIVERE

Gwenivere watched the cave's opening until the last captive emerged.

Dietrich was among them. Nayva too, as well as hundreds of others. Gwenivere didn't know any by name, but a few resembled her Hawks. Family members, then. People who had been taken, kidnapped, beaten. Forced to build Navar's empire.

When everyone was out, Gwenivere stepped back, far from the massive crowd, and released all the fire back into the cave.

If any Redeemers still pursued them, they'd have turned to embers. Their *auroras* would be ripped from their bodies.

Depleted, but still holding onto her Amulet's power, Gwenivere turned back to the enslaved.

No, not enslaved. Not anymore.

She turned back to her people.

"You're safe now," she said. "The Redeemers can no longer harm you."

To prove her point, she walked over to a stone just outside the cave entrance where Seera had deposited Navar. Gwenivere had found him, surrounded by more of his followers. She'd killed them as she had the others. Him, though, him she'd saved. She'd shouted for Seera, knowing that if she tried to grab the man, she'd melt him.

She didn't want him dead. Not quietly, in a corner, where no one would see.

She wanted her people to see the man who'd enslaved them.

She wanted to give them closure.

Seera had wrapped him in her claws, and flown back out the way she'd first come in. Gwenivere had asked her to find Dietrich, and though she'd not been able to hear the dragon's reply, she'd trusted her to bring them back.

"This is the man who imprisoned you," Gwenivere declared. With the flames unleashed, she pulled Navar up by his collar, and tossed him in front of her.

Seera had not been careful. Gwenivere could see a bone protruding from his leg.

"I endured his torment for only a few days. For some of you, it's been months. For some, it's been nearly a lifetime."

Her eyes found Dietrich's.

She didn't know what to say next. If the fury in his gaze was any indication of how the rest of them felt, Gwenivere imagined they'd want Navar dead, and they'd want him dead now.

He deserved it, certainly. He was a darkness upon the world. A disease. To be rid of him would be to rid the planet of a cancer that consumed.

Yet he was valuable. How much information could be pulled from him, if he was kept alive? How much more of the population might she and her people free, if only they knew how far his fingers of influence reached?

Gwenivere stared down at the man. She'd never killed

before today. In the blaze of the fight, she'd only wished to survive and escape. Now, despite wanting to be rid of him, she found she was only tired.

Still, there was a harsh truth she had to face:

She was Xenith's true queen. The man before her was an enemy to her nation.

It might not be today, but eventually, with a calm hand and a steady heart, she'd have to order his execution.

I will take no pleasure from that, she thought. Navar was an evil man, but he was old, and frail. She commanded the power of the divine.

Before she could speak again, Seera nudged her aside. The crowd, who'd pressed forward, suddenly backed up. The only person to dare step out was Dietrich. He looked different, somehow, like a man possessed. His eyes, which bore into Navar, seemed unfocused.

"For Zoran," he said.

Seera pushed Navar to his back, then grabbed his ankles, and bit down.

He screamed. The sound of bones breaking shattered through his cries.

Seera opened her mouth, then clamped down on his torso. She didn't bite all the way through. She only punctured the surface of his skin, then *called* fire, not as flames, but as black, burning smoke.

"For Savine," Dietrich said.

The dragon lifted her neck, thrust Navar up, then spat him onto the ground.

His cries stopped. His neck snapped.

It was only then that Seera *called* the flames, and turned Navar to ash.

It'd happened so quickly, Gwenivere hadn't had time to

stop it. Her mind had gone into shock. Her body too, she realized, for how paralyzed it'd suddenly become.

Attempting to ground herself, Gwenivere released a breath. With it, she finally, belatedly, stopped *calling* on her Amulet.

The act was met with agony. It was so swift, and so sudden, she hardly had a moment to cry out.

She fell to the ground. She gasped. Reeled. Her world began to spin. Her body submitted to pain, awful, excruciating, unexplainable pain.

And then her vision went black.

EPILOGUE

I

The worst of winter was over.

It was still dreadfully cold, but Elizabeth no longer inwardly cursed every time she needed to change her clothes or attempted to wash her hair.

Vixeen had left to visit the closest village. Such ventures had been few and far between for the last two months, but now, with ice becoming snow, and snow becoming frustrating puddles you slipped in rather than sunk into, paths could be traversed more easily. The sun stayed out for longer hours too, making travel less dangerous. The woman would be back in a few days' time, and hopefully she'd return with food, new clothing, and news about what'd been transpiring around the continent.

Elizabeth chose now to finally widen what she'd begun calling her safety hole. Vixeen had begged her not to call the dugout hiding place that, but seeing the spy so out of sorts had only solidified that the name needed to stick.

Maybe Elizabeth was more like her brothers than she thought.

Vixeen seemed relieved when it was finally warm enough to leave their hideout.

Truthfully, Elizabeth knew the spy would fret over her and miss her while she was away. You didn't spend nearly every waking moment with another person and get along with them wonderfully if you didn't at least somewhat like them. And Elizabeth was rather certain she and Vixeen more than liked each other. After experiencing terror and trivialities together, day in and day out, they were practically family.

Bored out of her mind with the spy gone, Elizabeth rolled back the rug that covered the floor, and got to work. She was surprised at how difficult the job was and how quickly her hands stung from the shovel. Still, there was little else to do. Pounding away, she managed to expand the ditch little by little. Sweat dripped down her brow and stung her eyes. It forced her to take breaks, if only to wipe the droplets from her skin.

It was during one of these breaks, sitting atop her bed and resting, that she allowed herself to take in the bloodstain on the floor. Usually the carpet hid it, which was fine by Elizabeth, as she wasn't fond of having to look at it. It brought to mind horrible images of Yvaine Barie tied up to the beam in the room's center, incurring the wrath of the late king.

The stain also reminded Elizabeth of the other one, just outside the cellar. It hadn't been so long ago that she'd visited the shack within the wheatgrass field and looked upon her family's deathplace.

Tired and still catching her breath, she studied the one at her feet now, marveling at how far it reached across the floor. If she had to guess, she'd estimate the stain was nearly the same size as the one in the shack.

That struck her as odd. Her family's bodies had all been stacked atop one another, but even then, the bloodstain in the shack was only a bit larger than the one beneath her, and Yvaine Barie had only been beaten, not killed. How could so much blood have spilled from a single person without killing them?

Unless...

Elizabeth bolted up. She'd not wanted to leave the cellar—she'd been ordered to never leave the cellar unless Vixeen was present and the surrounding area was clear—but she ran up the small stairway and pushed open the cellar's door. Light spilled onto her, blinding her for a moment, but she shielded her eyes from the sun, picked up her skirts, and ran to the shack.

She burst into the room. There was no wind today. She surveyed the deathplace of her family as she had all those months ago, eyes looking again to the dark stain on the wood. It reached across the floor. More than what was in the cellar, but of course there was more. Four people had died here. If she reduced the stain to a quarter of that size, it was comparable, maybe even smaller, than the bloodstain in the cellar.

Running back to her hideout, she looked at the surrounding area. If Yvaine Barie had lost that much blood, then surely some of the stairs would have bloodstains too. There might be a bloody handprint on the latch that led out of the cellar, or maybe even—if Elizabeth brushed away the snow—she'd find bloodstains on the nearly imperceptible cover that normally hid the cellar's entrance.

There were none.

There were no traces that Yvaine Barie had ever left the cellar.

I know who the spy is, she realized. She spun around, looking out across the wheat grass field, but of course, nobody was there.

She had no way to warn anyone.
She had no way to let Natalia know what was coming.

EPILOGUE
II

The Tiadorian ambassador had arrived.

Natalia met him as he came into Voradeen. She made sure knights and guards throughout the city were relegated to the paths the ambassador would be on. It wouldn't do to have anyone who'd lost a family member or loved one at the border attempting to enact uninformed vengeance. The printings would undoubtedly comment on the occasion, and the more vitriolic ones would claim that the palace cared more about important, foreign killers than the citizens of Xenith, but after the news of 'Gwenivere's' capture and exile, the majority of them would be feeling more charitable. The usual onslaught of hatred would be reduced to the equivalent of a suspicious glance.

To Natalia's surprise, Ambassador Dei-Sol was an exceptionally pleasant man. He was middle-aged with elegant clothing and a regal posture. It belied the low, rough sound of his voice, and the surprising charisma in his eyes. He seemed a person who'd endured much but allowed his experiences to educate him, rather than cause him to become bitter or hardened.

Natalia found she admired everything about him, from his garb and his demeanor to the warmth in his smile. Simply being around him made her want to be a better person. That was a rare thing. A new thing. She wasn't sure anyone besides Gerard Verigrad had ever made her feel that way.

Upon reaching the palace, she offered him the teas Becca had taught her about. The exchange went well, though it lacked any really depth or momentum, as she and Dei-Sol both seemed preoccupied with getting a grasp on the other more than anything else.

Natalia wanted to say more beyond general trivialities, but the ambassador said he was tired from his travels and wished to retire until their meeting with the Treaty of Five.

"Of course," Natalia said. "Let me show you to your rooms. If they are not to your liking, feel free to let myself or any of the knights attending you know, and we will find better accommodations."

"Your hospitality is appreciated. Trust me, though, Queen Regent, we in Tiador live with very little. Whatever you offer will be more than enough."

Natalia didn't know if the statement was one of condemnation or if he was simply stating a fact. Regardless, it sent her on a mad hunt to gain more knowledge. Rather than sleeping, she stayed up, looking through everything she could on Tiador —everything *else* she could, besides what she'd read leading up to the ambassador's arrival—and tried to memorize all her mind could hold.

Though she'd not wanted to stop to eat or drink, she knew it prudent to keep her mind sharp and her energy up. Reluctantly, she put her books down, much to Sir Nicolas's relief, as the candlelight she'd used all throughout the night kept him from sleeping. He'd hoped to nap a bit before the meeting started, but as she dressed, she relayed various facts to him. Teaching someone was the best way to retain information. By the time the foreign dignitaries met, Nicolas would be the third most knowledge person in the room on Tiador, after the Tiadorian himself, and Natalia.

Despite her preference for lightweight gowns, she'd discovered Tiadorian nobles often dressed with a mix of fine fabrics and armor. Adopting the style, she dawned a light blue dress embroidered with gold leaves along the front, the size of the leaves ranging from small to large as they swept down to the floor. The dress flared only slightly, a contrast to her golden armor bodice, and the tight metal around her shoulders and neck. Her hair, parted in the middle and pulled back from her face, was ornamented with small pieces of gold, bringing out the occasional matching strands among her silver and white hair.

Pulled back locks, she'd read, symbolized one eager to see unimpeded. It was often associated with a person who wished to take in the world and learn. Apt pupils were drawn with such styles, or newly appointed royals. Natalia thought it a fitting thing for her to wear, then, hoping Dei-Sol would recognize her appearance for what it was: a willingness to meet with him not from a place of judgment but curiosity.

She'd sent runners down to inform Aden's servants on how best to dress him. Though he'd not be talking much during the meeting, his presentation still mattered. It had to look as though the boy embraced the path to respectability, rather than appearing as a spoiled child playing at king.

As for the Treaty of Five members, Natalia didn't bother providing them with guidance. Commandant Hedford was a lost cause, as the man was always brash and never gave anyone much respect. Edifor was an ambassador himself, so he likely already knew how best to speak and dress and act. Vanessa never seemed particularly interested in anyone or anything. She talked little at meetings and only seemed keen on keeping herself abreast of each situation. The Arctic's politics were a bit confusing to Natalia, but she understood that Vanessa, a baroness, could never rule her country, despite being a daughter of the current queen, all because she'd left her borders. Thus, only her children could be eligible for the throne, so long as they themselves never left their home and their lands brought in the most amount of wealth. Vanessa, then, would pay attention for selfish reasons, but she didn't fear Tiador, nor did she care if Dei-Sol liked her. She only wished to wring what she could from the meeting, and figure out how best to capitalize on that knowledge.

That left Yvaine.

All Natalia asked of her mother was that she didn't launch into any accusations. She could say and think whatever she wanted of the ambassador and his country, but she needed to keep her usual abrasive attitude to herself.

Don't mess this up for me, Natalia silently pleaded. She sent the thought in the direction of her mother's rooms, then turned from the mirror she'd been standing in front of, looking to Nicolas.

"What do you think? Suitable?"

He blinked tired eyes but managed a small smile.

"I don't think you've ever looked so regal."

Natalia tried not to smile back, but she lost the battle. The corners of her lips lifted.

She was nervous, but she was *excited* nervous. For the first time in months, she actually had an opportunity to change things for the better. The news of Gwenivere's capture and exile had lifted the spirits within Voradeen in a way that was nearly tangible. With the Sadiyans credited for her capture, the tension between them and Xens within the city had nearly evaporated. Even Natalia's worst critics seemed to sing happier tunes.

She also, finally, had the opportunity to end the trade ban. With that, she could stimulate Xenith's economy, as well as help the sick. More money would also mean more ways to help the poor throughout the nation, as well as those who still needed their homes repaired. The squire program could be expanded, which would lead to more knights, which would lead to more people monitoring crime throughout both the upper and lower districts.

If everything went well with Dei-Sol, Natalia could also potentially expand trade to the Far West and bring home the soldiers that'd been stationed at the border. Those soldiers could then take jobs that helped rebuild the city or they could stay within Xenith's ranks and enlist to help in other cities, like Sarabai, to the east.

I can see why Dorian always liked this, she thought. For the first time since becoming Queen Regent, Natalia felt like she truly had power. Not just power. Hope. She was seeing light breaking through storm clouds.

"We have one stop to make before the meeting," she said. "Care to join me in the dungeons?"

Nicolas made a sound of disgust.

She poked his arm. "Agreed."

Having discovered that Vel had been Anastasia's 'spy,' Natalia had possessed little reason to continue interrogating Azar. Clearly what he'd told her regarding a shape-shifter among the palace had been a made-up story fed to him by the

Prianthian noblewoman. Its only purpose had been to sew fear and doubt—a purpose that'd worked for too long.

Still, he had his uses. He'd thrown a weapon during the conference that'd been meant to come across as Tiadorian, and Natalia doubted her western neighbor appreciated the act.

As a gift to Dei-Sol, she would hand Azar over and allow him to be interrogated as the Tiadorians saw fit. Maybe they could pose questions of him that Natalia hadn't thought to ask. Maybe they would kill him. It didn't matter. So long as Dei-Sol saw the gesture of goodwill for what it was, Natalia would be happy.

Making the detour, she hurried to the dungeon. The guards standing post nodded in acknowledgment as she and Nicolas approached.

"I wish for the prisoner Azar to be made presentable," she said. "See that the task is done quickly."

The guards looked to each other, then back at her.

"Apologies, Queen Regent," one of them said. Natalia thought she remembered his name was Erivahn.

"Apologies for what?"

"You . . . you must be in shock. Sometimes that can happen seeing someone die."

Natalia frowned. She shared a look with Nicolas, but he seemed just as perplexed as she was.

"What are you talking about?"

"Azar died," the other knight said. "You were the one to report it."

"You're mistaken. I haven't seen the prisoner recently."

"We have it here in the logs." Erivahn pulled a board and parchment that hung just to the side of the dungeon's entrance. He handed it over to her and Nicolas.

Her name was signed, as was the time.

"Were you the ones posted when this happened?" she asked, concerned.

"No, Queen Regent. Would you like us to get the other logs of who was stationed that day?"

"Yes, please do. Nicolas, stay back and get this sorted. Just to be clear, though . . ." She swallowed, steeling her nerves. "The prisoner Azar is, in fact, dead?"

Erivahn nodded. "I'm afraid so. His body was released from the dungeons the day it happened and brought to the Temple of the Stone so he might *ascend* in peace. It's what's done to prisoners who are never given trials."

Natalia nodded. She was glad now she'd not promised Azar to Dei-Sol and had merely planned to surprise the ambassador an act of good faith. Even so, her prior excitement grew sour.

"Even if it interrupts the meeting, approach me when you have this resolved," she told Nicolas. "I have to go or I'll be late. You know the room?"

Her knight assured her he did, and they parted ways.

Not allowing the bad news to bring her down, Natalia forced her tired mind to run through everything she'd learned about Tiador. She reminded herself of their greetings, the words or terms they considered offensive, what their religious beliefs were, when it was appropriate to speak, and how best to interject if one had something useful to add to a conversation.

She ran through every useful fact she could until she'd arrived at the assigned meeting room. She took a deep breath, smoothed down her skirts, and entered.

Surprisingly, everyone was already in attendance. Though her detour hadn't caused her to be tardy, she'd still not anticipated she'd be the last noble to arrive. Her mother, Hedford, Vanessa, Edifor, and even Aden were all seated, each engaged in pleasant conversation, save the king, who watched with curious eyes. Only Peter was missing, but he arrived a moment later, satchel over his shoulder and notebook in hand. Natalia looked to him as he entered, wanting to apologize that this meeting was only happening because they were holding his brother as collateral over the border.

He pointedly ignored her. Adjusting his satchel's strap, he found his seat, which was separate from the rest. It was the only one that wasn't around the long table in the room's center.

This time, Natalia hadn't been relegated to listener alongside him. That small difference felt symbolic.

Forcing a smile, she greeted each of the attendees.

With everyone present, they agreed to start early.

"I'd like to begin by saying that my personal knight may need to deliver news to me at some point," she said. "If he does, I offer my apologies for having to excuse myself, but the information is pertinent to the meeting and concerns everyone.

"Directness is valued in Tiador, so in accordance with the ways of our most recent guest, I think it best we launch immediately into the matter of the trade ban with Sadie.

"Ambassador Dei-Sol, the rest of us here decided to forgo making a decision on whether to end or keep the trade ban until we'd had the opportunity to meet with you. Given the sanctions placed on Tiador after the War of Fire, we understand that reworking previous trade agreements with your country might be of interest."

Dei-Sol nodded, then provided each of them duplicates of a message written by his ruler. It was in depth, more so than any of the financial documents and records kept by Xen advisers. It provided, in detail, all the ways in which restrictions over the last thirty-plus years had impacted their people, ranging from reduced access to the East's cures, building materials needed to rebuild cities destroyed during the war, illnesses that'd kept people from working, and forests that'd been burned down, leaving them without vital resources for construction and food. Wildlife had suffered, impacting their abilities to hunt. Predators that'd once kept away looked for food inside small villages or from traveling caravans.

The message was clear: the War of Fire had not ended for Tiador when it had ended for Xenith, Mesidia, and their allies. It still raged, though it'd become a slow, lingering death, rather than a quick one.

"We do not feel we can progress from *this* point," Dei-Sol said, steepling his hands atop the table. "We must make up for the wrongs placed on us from decades prior."

"But these demands are preposterous!" Hedford slapped his parchment back onto the table. "You're insisting that every one of our countries provides you with 30 percent of what we've earned over the last thirty years."

"Money was stolen from us before the War of Fire," Dei-Sol answered calmly. "That war started because you all became rich off of the trade meant to come into our country. It was known we were a peaceful people, unable to fight back. You forced anyone trading goods into my home to pay you exorbitant fees. By the time they reached us, much of the goods we'd already paid for went back into your hands. You crippled our economy."

"And you burned our fields," Yvaine said. "You put salt in the soil so a number of our crops could no longer grow. These were the products of war. You chose violence, rather than reworking trade deals, and we defeated you. Why should we now face the consequences for those actions?"

Hedford passionately agreed. Vanessa and Edifor watched, interested, and Aden sat silently.

"It is hard to rework deals," Dei-Sol said, "when the ones in place aren't being honored."

"Then let us make new ones," Natalia said. "Ambassador, we wanted to present you with the opportunity to have your nation be reopened to trade with us. What if we reopened trade not only with you, but with Sadie as well? To compensate for the loss of trade over the years, we can guarantee that any goods transported from Sadie to you will not be taxed in our lands. Traveling merchants and traders will be given discounted stays at any of our inns, across our countries."

She looked to the others. They nodded their agreement.

"Sadie had invaluable resources," she continued. "I assure you: They are better than what any of our countries have. We can work through the details of this agreement, and you can write to your king tonight and see what specifications he'd wish documented in a deal, but would this serve as at least a start in repairing the damage caused to your country?"

Dei-Sol laced his fingers together. He sat on the information, and the room seemed to collectively hold its breath.

When he nodded, Natalia silently released a sigh of relief.

"Then we're in agreement," she said. "We end the trade ban with Sadie?"

It was put to a vote. They all said yes.

Peter, sitting by the room's only window, documented the monumental moment.

"There will be much to discuss," Natalia said, attempting to hide her glee. "We can't determine anything concrete today with the new trade deals, especially not without consulting Sadie first—which might be difficult, given their current predicament—but Ambassador Dorian might be able to work with the nation to relay their wants to us, and ours to them.

"For now, I think it best we determine what we'd like out of this new trade deal for each of our respective nations. Those of you representing your rulers, you can pass this information along to them after this meeting is adjourned. How long do you believe it will take to receive information back for each of your nations? Baroness, what say you?"

Natalia wrote down the estimated times for the Arctic, Theatia, and Yendor. Before she could write the same thing down for Tiador, a knock sounded, and Nicolas was allowed in.

"Excuse me," Natalia said. "This pertains to the interruption I warned about earlier."

"I think this wonderful start calls for celebration," Yvaine said, beckoning for Sir Maximus to bring over the wine glasses placed on a table in the room's back. "I was going to wait until further into the meeting, but this seems as fine a moment as ever."

Dipping her head, Natalia thanked her mother for the momentary distraction. She rose from her seat and met Nicolas by the door.

"What did the knight logs show?" she asked quietly, not wanting to be overheard. "Were they men who don't know what I look like?"

Nicolas shook his head. "They're knights who are normally stationed at the dungeon. They're absolutely familiar with you."

"I wasn't there," she insisted. "That wasn't even my handwriting. Could it have been Vel? Before she left?"

"That's the odd part." Nicolas leaned in closer. "The time that was documented was when you and Vel were both in the palace's hidden corridors. It couldn't have been her." He swallowed, and Natalia noticed a bead of sweat at his brow. "I . . . I think someone murdered the prisoner. And I think they somehow convinced the knights it was you."

Natalia fought the urge to lean on Nicolas. Her legs suddenly felt numb. Her stomach clenched.

Vel had been the spy. She'd confirmed it. There was no shape-shifter. Even if there were, they couldn't have passed as Natalia. Though there were gaps in her knowledge regarding the lore of the creatures, all accounts agreed that they needed the blood of whomever they were impersonating. Natalia hadn't sustained any injuries since being Queen Regent, not since the day of the conference, and even then, the only person who'd seen to her wounds was...

Natalia turned around. Everyone at the table sat back in their seats, their conversations having lapsed into something less formal. They all were drinking the wine Yvaine had poured for them, all save Aden, who Maximus had refused to let partake.

Yvaine herself was at the end of the table, near Natalia's seat. Her hand was lifted to pour her a drink as well, but it seemed frozen, perpetually hovering over Natalia's wine glass.

Slowly, her breaths shallow, Natalia stepped toward her mother.

Before she reached her, Hedford, having already drained his glass, began to vomit.

Peter threw his satchel and notebook down and rushed over to the man. Maximus hurried to get him water. Just as he set the glass down, Dei-Sol too began to vomit.

Vanessa was next.

Then Edifor.

Natalia would be as well, if her mother had managed to pour her glass and convinced her to drink. Instead, with everyone sick around them, Yvaine continued to stand frozen, face pained, her hand continuing to hang over the glass.

Nicolas pulled Natalia back, pushing her behind him. The vomit turned to blood. Peter, who'd been trying to offer consoling words, sprang back, cursing. Maximus lifted Aden up and made for the door.

"Get him to a healer!" Nicolas shouted, opening the door for him. "Get other healers in here—now! Send more knights!"

He tried to push Natalia out too, but she stood in place. She couldn't look away. She couldn't stop watching as Hedford's skin became red, then purple, then blue. He reached up to his chest before collapsing from his seat.

The same things seemed to happen in slow motion to the others.

Nicolas was shouting something, but Natalia didn't hear him. She saw Peter no longer paying any mind to Hedford, but instead trying to help Dei-Sol.

Yes, of course he'd try to help the ambassador. If Dei-Sol died, that meant his brother would be in danger.

"Pour my glass," Natalia said, approaching her mother. The woman still hadn't moved.

"Do as Anastasia ordered."

Yvaine looked up at her. Her eyes, normally blue, shifted to a deep brown red.

"I . . . can't," she managed. Her voiced seemed strained. Deep.

It didn't sound feminine.

"Why?" Natalia asked. Hedford had stopped moving. The others thrashed, grabbing at their throats.

"The Ageless." Her mother—or the thing that'd taken her mother's face—began to undulate. "In this form . . . I . . . can't."

Nicolas finally managed to shove Natalia back. He did so just as Yvaine's face melted away. Her skin shifted. Her shoulders grew. A guttural yell escaped as she collapsed, and her torso lengthened.

In less than a heartbeat, Yvaine Barie was gone. In her place stood a man Natalia had never seen.

"Victor?" she guessed. She remembered the name Azar had

given. At the sound of it, the shape-shifter looked up. He'd seemed pained before, but now he looked sorrowful.

"I'm sorry," he said. He pulled a dagger from a sheath at his side and lunged for her.

Peter struck him from behind with the chair he'd dragged Dei-Sol from. Nicolas pulled the sword from his side and deflected the strike.

The shape-shifter was fast. Inhumanely fast. He ducked from Peter's attack, turned, and grabbed the chair, yanking it away. Peter stumbled back, but it wasn't him Victor aimed for. He threw the chair at Nicolas, surprising him, then threw the knife.

It struck true, landing in Nicolas's chest. The knight made to yank it out, but Natalia stopped him, fearful he'd make the wound worse.

"Stop!" she yelled, as much to her knight as the creature in front of her. "If you're sorry, don't do this!"

"I can't," he said. "My commands..."

His body returned to the shape of her mother. Nicolas collapsed in Natalia's arms. She fell with him to the floor, grabbing his sword in case her mother—the shape-shifter—came for her again.

The creature continued to change. It seemed stuck in a mocking loop, one second holding her mother's face, the next, a young man barely past his twentieth winter.

He screamed.

Natalia continued holding Nicolas, horrified. Petrified.

For all the research she'd done, nothing had prepared her for this morbid, macabre spectacle.

As the members of the Treaty ceased their struggling, so too did the being in front of her. It settled on its true form as Maximus returned, along with healers, and dozens of knights.

Growling, the shape-shifter ran toward the window, broke through the glass, and hurled itself off the balcony.

The healers tried to take Nicolas away. Natalia refused to let him go. They began treating him there, where she could watch over him. She didn't want to let him out of her sight.

She didn't ever want to let him out of her sight again.

Some of the knights ran to the shattered window. They returned empty handed. Maximus crouched on the floor beside her, informing her that the king was safe. He said something else, about wine and poison, but Natalia barely heard it.

It'd happened again.

First Gerard. Now this. Just as it had before, people had fallen to their knees before her, clasped to their chests, and breathed their last breaths.

Not just people. Ambassadors. A baroness. A commandant.

There was no false blame to be placed this time. No escape. Natalia had wrongfully assigned fault before, and something sinister and wicked had decided this was her punishment. To live the moment again, but as the cruelest of nightmares, with her mother at the center.

Not her mother. She knew that now. Her mother had died months ago.

It'd only been a short time before when Natalia had been proud of herself for purging her mind of her mother's influence. She'd not realized that those voices in her head, those echoes of her mother's chastisement, and scolding, and twisted arrogance, were the last remnants she'd had of her.

Now they were gone. Her mother was gone. She'd died alone in a cellar. Natalia had never freed her.

"They're all dead, I'm afraid," a healer reported. They'd tried to resuscitate Dei-Sol, Hedford, Vanessa, and Edifor. Natalia wasn't sure why. It was obvious they weren't coming back.

Beside her, Nicolas was being assured he was going to make it. Maximus sat on his other side, holding the hand Natalia didn't. She hadn't even realized she'd been clinging to her knight so tightly.

Peter was there. Eyes wide. Lost.

"What . . ." He licked his lips, then began shaking. "What now?"

Natalia didn't answer.

She couldn't.

She had absolutely no idea what to do.

CHARACTER LIST

A compilation of individuals from various kingdoms, taken from the letters of Ambassador Dorian and Prince Abaddon, reports from Dravian Valcor to Pierre Laighless, notes from the High Council of Eve, Peace Gathering reservations from Sir Charles of Xenith, meeting records between Natalia Barie and Veladee Verigrad, journal entries by Dietrich Haroldson, studies on Abra'am by X'odia Daer'dee, and unknown communications between a rebel group known as the Hawks.

Abaddon Haroldson: king of Sadie
Aden Verigrad: ruler select of Xenith
Alanna Verkev: daughter-heir of Prianthia
Alexandria Verkev: royalty of Prianthia
Alkane: Guardian to the Shield of Eve
Anastasia Verkev: royalty of Prianthia
Antigone: woman residing in Sarabai
Avendar: knight of Xenith
Azar: writer working for the Vines of Voradeen
Azgar: sailor residing in Riverdee
Becca: chambermaid in the

Voradeen palace
Bernard Barie VII: duke of Mesidia
Brelain: healer residing in the towns of the Dividing Wall
Bronal: Evean captain of the Seagull
Callum: city guard of Riverdee
Cara: young resident of Riverdee
Catherine al'Murtagh: mother of al'Murtagh siblings, sister of Pierre Laighless
Charles: personal knight of Gerard Verigrad
Cid Orloff: member of the Evean High Council
Cillian: owner of the Dusty Boot
Culter Sandborne: head watchman of Sadie
Daensla: mysterious Sadiyan woman tied to Dietrich Haroldson
Dar: city guard of Riverdee
Deladrine: Sadiyan oracle
Dietrich Haroldson: elder prince of Sadie
Dorian Cliffborne: ambassador of Mesidia
Dravian Valcor: head of the Elite
Edifor: ambassador of Yendor
Elizabeth al'Murtagh: Mesidian royalty, cousin to Roland Laighless
Fiona Collinson: wealthy woman residing in the towns of the Dividing Wall
Garron Hillborne: personal knight to Gwenivere Verigrad
Gerard Verigrad: king of Xenith
Gregor: man residing in Sarabai
Gregory Collinson: husband of Fiona
Gwenivere Verigrad: princess of Xenith, Guardian to the Amulet of Eve
Harold Rorikson: king of Sadie
Hedford: commandant of Theatia
Joel al'Murtagh: husband to Catherine, father to the al'Murtagh siblings
Lenore Daer: queen of Sadie
Marie Hill: late wife of Garron Hillborne
Markeem the Mute: third in command of Mesidian Elite
Maximus Hillborne: personal knight to Aden Verigrad
Merlin: personal Elite to Roland Laighless

Natalia Barie: Queen Regent of Xenith
Navar: leader of the Redeemers
Nayva: healer residing near Sarabai
Nicolai Verkev: royalty of Prianthia
Nicolas Hillborne: knight of Xenith
Odin Iceborne: fourth in command of Mesidian Elite
Pasha Verkev: assassinated royalty of Prianthia
Peter al'Murtagh: Mesidian royalty, cousin to Roland Laighless
Pierre Laighless: king of Mesidia
Ravel: Evean sailor of the Seagull
Rellor Bordinsua: second in command of Mesidian Elite
Rokinoff Verkev: royalty of Prianthia
Roland Laighless: prince of Mesidia, Guardian to the Amulet of Eve
Rosalie Laighless: queen of Mesidia
Rose Verigrad: late queen of Xenith
Rynara Stone: woman residing in Sarabai, Xenith
Samuel Sandborne: healer residing in Sovereignty, Sadie
Sasha: woman residing in Sarabai
Savine: dragon residing in the mountains Dividing Wall
Scavol: man residing in Riverdee
Seera: dragon residing in the mountains Dividing Wall
Sehan Sand: watchman of Sadie
Teniv: a successful tradeswoman and shop owner
Vahd'eel: mysterious Evean man
Vanessa: baroness of the Arctic
Veladee Verigrad: cousin to Gwenivere Verigrad
Victor of the Black: rumored assassin and shapeshifter of the Redeemers
Vixeen: Victorian soldier and friend of Dorian Cliffborne
William al'Murtagh: Mesidian royalty, cousin to Roland Laighless
X'odia Daer'dee: Evean woman, daughter of Alkane
Yvaine Barie: leader select of Mesidia
Zain: boy residing in the towns of the Dividing Wall

Zelhada Sand: watchman of Sadie
Zoran: dragon keeper residing in the mountains of the Dividing Wall
Zuri: a serving woman at The Dusty Boot

ACKNOWLEDGMENTS

Since the release of my first book, I have lost both my father and my grandmother. Both were tremendous influences in my life. They showed me unconditional love, support, and joy. I miss them dearly.

Though I continue to feel their absence, I am fortunate to have others in my life who have made this book possible. I owe them all my gratitude.

Thank you to my husband. You will forever by my best friend and favorite person.

Thank you to my mom. Seeing you happy is a highlight of the last few years.

Thank you to my friends (especially Rodger and Jashana). Each and every one of you is both a gift to this world and to me.

For all the people who helped bring this book to life, including the artists Madison, Inna, and Ari, and the always wonderful editor Mollie, this book would not only not exist without you, but it would be a far inferior version if you'd not worked so hard on it.

Lastly, thank you to everyone who has supported me, whether it be through words of encouragement, reading and geeking out over books with me, subscribing to my work and my patreon, or taking a chance on my writing. It means more than you could know.

ABOUT THE AUTHOR

Elliot Brooks lives in Arizona with her husband Sean and her dog Luna Bear.